THE AVENUE

James Lawless

WORDSONTHESTREET

First published in 2010 by
Wordsonthestreet
Six San Antonio Park,
Salthill,
Galway, Ireland.
web: www.wordsonthestreet.com
email: publisher@wordsonthestreet.com

A catalogue record for this book is available from the British Library.

ISBN   978-1-907017-02-5

Cover design, layout and typesetting: Wordsonthestreet

Printed and bound in the UK

THE AVENUE

About the author

James Lawless was born in Dublin and divides his time between Kildare and West Cork.

A first novel, *Peeling Oranges* was published in 2007. His book on modern poetry, *Clearing The Tangled Wood: Poetry as a way of seeing the world*, for which he received the Cecil Day Lewis arts bursary award, was published in 2009, as was his second novel *For Love of Anna*.

He may be contacted on Amazon.com at his writer profile page.

To Margaret

'Who now is homeless builds himself no house.
Who is alone now will long remain so,
will stay awake, and read, and write long letters,
and in the avenues, when the leaves are drifting,
wander anxiously.'

from *Autumn Day* by Rainer Maria Rilke
(trans. Desmond Fennell)

Autumn. A time of shedding. The Americans call it the fall but most of the leaves, although russet and nicely golden now, are still on the trees. The avenue retains the residue of summer, kids playing out late, neighbours mowing lawns or soaking up the last of the sunshine at their porch doors, no frost as yet.

I move away from the bedroom window and enter the study where I continue my reading of *The Name of the Rose* by Umberto Eco. Adso had encountered the beautiful and terrible maiden. But after his knowledge of the girl he understood the abyss. I know exactly what Adso means by that. I read a lot. I've always read ever since my mother died a long time ago. I always carry a story around in my head. It gives me a universe that I can control, that I can terminate at any time simply by snapping covers shut. She started me off as a baby on her knee, showing me pictures from the picture books, putting words where there were no words and then asking me to tell her what I saw in the picture to make a story. I unfathomed tales of chivalry and knights in armour defending damsels in distress. And I had the consolation of knowing that she was always there at the end no matter how difficult or frightening the adventure had been.

But there is another reason why I have frequent recourse to my study. It's to do with Myrtle, my wife who is forever bossing me about (and sometimes doing more than that). So I take off whenever I can and place myself behind the covers of a book and experience – even if it is vicariously – all the vagaries of life without life's drawbacks. The book is my only affirmation in the world, unlike Myrtle and her friend Ida who feed off one another and take their mutual affirmations for granted as they cut down the common foe with their sabre tongues. I'm the common foe, needless to add or at least part of it, for the foe to them is anyone with an appendage hanging between his legs.

I daydream more like a lost adolescent than a fully grown man.

Closing the study door acts as a Dolby to muffle Myrtle's stentorian commands to put out the bin or bring in the clothes or look at the state of this or the state of that. Myrtle gathers her edicts and comments like a quiver of arrows which she fires in rapid succession before slamming the front door, as she invariably does, and going over to Ida with whom she consorts most evenings.

The study window looks out on the back garden. Dusk is falling now and the leaves are looking doleful. The garden has a lot of shrubs and a few trees – deciduous mainly – despite its diminutive size. A plastic football lies half hidden (I can just make it out) under the privet near the shed. A breeze makes the leaves give a little shudder trying to force an early fall.

I used to garden once but I have little interest in it now ever since what was done to my knee. I can't kneel anymore. Dad always said – in his lucid moments – that gardening was like praying, that you can't do it properly without kneeling. Or he would say rather unsympathetically, 'A gardener who can't kneel is like a horse who can't run. You shoot him or put him out to grass.' That's what my father said and I wondered about the way he used the word 'grass', but then he ought to know having worked as a professional gardener for most of his life. Well, I'm off the grass now so to speak. I don't miss it, the work, I mean. I still like looking at plants and trees but I have my answer ready when Myrtle complains about the dishevelled borders or the weeds choking the annuals. Weeding must be one of the most futile of all activities: you remove something from the earth and it returns to torment you at the sky's whim whenever it decides to throw down a little shine or rain, and the weed you thought you had strangled just shoots straight up at you again. 'And look at my father,' I said to Myrtle, 'all his life gardening, and what good did it do him?' And then I felt guilty for using my father merely to buttress an argument.

The truth of the matter is that I could still make an effort, at gardening I mean, but what's the point of cultivating a garden when one is far away from Eden? So I use the knee as an excuse. It has something to do with the treachery of roses. That's what I said to Dad when he asked me what happened, when he saw me lying in a pool of blood on the sitting-room floor. I wouldn't tell him anymore than that. Just an accident, I said when he pressed me.

Sometimes I think of sleep as anaesthesia and it makes me fearful. That's why I always have a glass of water by my bed. It's like I'm afraid something is going to take my breath away. It was because of my knee. I never wanted to admit it was Myrtle's doing – it's not really a manly thing to admit I suppose, I mean a woman beating a man. But she did it all right. It was in the early days. I remember I was bringing my cup and plate to the sink. She was in a bad mood; she'd had some row with Ida. She had the ironing board out at the time, taking up the whole kitchen, and she backed into me (with her increasing rotundity), knocking the cup off the plate and it smashed on the floor. 'Pick it up,' she said. 'Pick it up yourself,' I said. It wasn't the first time I stood up to her. I was beginning to cotton on to her ways. But this time she was livid. So I went into the living room to let her cool off and I sat down on the sofa and started reading a book. She followed me with the iron. I never saw a woman mad before. She was foaming at the mouth and she lashed at my right knee with the iron, and kept lashing at it until the kneecap was good and shattered.

After the anaesthetic I came to prematurely. It was a terrible feeling. The nausea. All I knew was that I had to get out of the place, get air. I remembered, when I was four or five I was given gas for the removal of my tonsils. I had asthma at the time. I was always told to close my mouth. My mother and teachers told me an open mouth was considered imbecilic, but I could never figure out the connection between the mouth and the brain. I mean think of eyes open, hands open, ears; there was no taboo associated with them, just the mouth. Maybe that's why I couldn't breathe through my mouth when it mattered. No one told me to breathe through my mouth as the mask was put over my face. I fought the ether like I was fighting for my life, as I breathed it in through my nostrils, the overpowering smell lodged somewhere permanently inside my nose and it rises every time I near a hospital.

So that's why I guess I panicked after the knee job and had to get out. I gave some young fellow Myrtle's bottle of Lucozade for tying my shoelaces – oh yes Myrtle brought me Lucozade, and big black grapes. The young fellow helped me onto a crutch, and I hobbled out the push door – there was no one there to stop me, and I remember the nausea was worse than the pain and I felt the night cold and welcome on my face. But I wound up in a dead end lane where an old shawled woman sat in a puddle of rainwater with her bottle of porter and I knew there was no other way to go but back.

It wasn't that I was timid, for I had held my own against school bullies. No, it's just this was uncharted territory. Because of my mother, I venerated women. Myrtle's action was not part of my script. I could never raise my hand to her, not through fear, but through respect for her gender. And Myrtle knew this. I simply did not know how to respond.

So all I could do was glare impotently at her as she chatted away, as if I hadn't gone anywhere, as if everything were fine, and she chatted to the nurse and the other patients as well and said it was a nasty fall coming down that hill and landing on the sharp rock as I did, and then she smoothed my pillows like a dutiful wife.

It's Tuesday evening and Myrtle shouts up to me that she is going over to Ida's. Unmarried Ida Hourigan with her boyish hips and flat chest; she smokes cheroots and walks straight and erect in tight jeans without the undulating stride characteristic of most females. Her mother was from London. She married a Dublin builder and they came over here to escape the Blitz. I remember my father, who was in England for a brief period during the War, talking about her and her tales of the bombing. There was also some mention of a sister in Liverpool. Ida is one of the toughest wags on the avenue. I can never get away with a criticism of her though when Myrtle is around. Tuesday night is bingo night and Myrtle and Ida never miss a week, or so they say. I mean I never thought of it before. I just presume that's where they go. You see the women in their coats and headscarves and handbags heading down the avenue in droves, every Tuesday night at twenty to eight. Saint Anthony's Hall – what a name to call it, as if the saint would find money for them. Call out the numbers and then call on the saint and then bingo! Not that I ever see any of Myrtle's winnings, mind. She keeps those things to herself but you'll always know she's made a kill when you see her going around sporting a new rigout. Funny, whatever about Myrtle, I just can't picture Ida in such an environment. Too staid for her. Not enough aggro. She likes aggro, likes stirring things up does Ida.

Through the study window I see the night fall. A few early stars and a half moon have appeared in the sky. I get up from my desk and am about to draw the curtains when a light goes on in a top window of the house opposite. I don't know the people over there. With the exception of the wags, most of us know few people beyond our own avenue or even, as in my case, *on* our own avenue. At least that's what I presume. Not knowing is interesting though in that it gives room for one to speculate, to imagine. To see people from a distance mythologises them into one's own little dreams. It's a bit like when you turn the TV volume down and create your own dialogue for the gesturing actors on the screen. I do that a lot especially for some Hollywood soaps whose dialogues always seem to be inane and too loud. Myrtle orders me to turn off the TV saying that I'm wasting it, using it like that. Or else she tells me to turn up the volume. Myrtle likes soaps; she watches old video reruns of *Dallas*. 'I know you don't call it real life,' she said, when I questioned her about the series once. 'Imagine JR living on the avenue, that would be a laugh. I only watch it for the glamour, to see the fashions and the clothes.' But she *doesn't* only watch it for the glamour and the clothes. I know that. I've heard her talk at length and with fascination to Ida about JR's extramarital affairs.

The room across is lighted as if in expectation of someone. I can make out a bed and an ivory-coloured wardrobe and what looks like the back of a mirror perched near the window.

A tall blond girl in a black leather jacket and jeans enters the room. She is perhaps in her late teens. She removes her jacket and a T-shirt underneath and then sheds the jeans which leaves her standing in what apparently is a pink bikini. I turn off the light in the study and view her from the darkness. I feel a rush of heat to my face.

One is forced to ask is this girl *conscious* that her blind is not pulled down? Is she *on* something? Is she an exhibitionist? Is she playing on the voyeuristic in men, in people? Girls in a Dublin suburb don't go around shedding their clothes in lighted windows. They are not conditioned that way. They are known as demure among other nationalities. Or perhaps that's an antiquated opinion, and Myrtle and Ida are certainly exceptions to that rule. But then she may be of another nationality. Suburbs are becoming multi-ethnic, what with Ida being of English stock and the two Black students and the Bosnian refugees living at the end of the avenue, it's becoming ever more difficult to generalise.

She starts to dance presumably to the accompaniment of some music, judging by the way she swings her arms and gyrates her hips and bends and turns and shakes her long mane.

I stare through my dark rectangular screen and try to construct a character for this silent dancer. Give her a name. Call her Sandra. I imagine girls named Sandra as blond. A young girl on the avenue with a blond doll in a pram told me to say hello to Sandra, to shake her hand, and she forced a squeak out of the doll by pressing her torso down to meet her legs.

'I'm home,' Myrtle shouts.

I long to tell someone about what I saw but Myrtle is not the one. She would just call me a pervert. Or I could ask her if she knows the people in the house directly behind us, but I don't want my Sandra coarsened by Myrtle's gossip. I feel excited like a child holding a secret.

In bed beside Myrtle I think of Sandra just a stone's throw away in her room. I hear a sound next door. The sound becomes a shout and Browne's dog starts whining.

Sometimes, if I've brought her something to eat like a bar of chocolate, Myrtle lets me hold her wrist – the thinnest part of her, which reminds me of the time when she was not quite so voluminous – and I might doze off that way, but if I attempt anything more she says, 'Where would you be going at this hour of the night?'

The next night, before getting into bed and perhaps not realising that I'm speaking out loud, I say, 'I must check the study.'

Myrtle looks up from her *Hello* magazine. 'What do you mean, check the study?'

'Did I say that?'

'You're Frank the Loop all right.'

'Ah there it is,' I say, picking up a book from the bedside locker. It was one I had read already but I decided to make do with it for that night.

Sandra is getting mixed up in some Limbo region between my dream and real worlds. She is like Eve, tempting me. Maybe I should have called her Eve but then I'd have no one to compare her with. Besides, I always thought of Eve as a brunette. As I think of Tuesday night I begin to see a pattern forming. I mean every other night the blind across is drawn. It is only on Tuesday nights that the blind is raised and Sandra appears to do her act. And it is on Tuesday nights that Myrtle goes out. She is the crusader venturing out to the Holy Land of Bingo and this girl has been sent to test me. But Myrtle has me locked into a chastity belt, a male version of course, fitted with a clamp which descends to grasp the penis tightly at the slightest hint of an erection.

The strange thing is Myrtle was quite a temptress when we first met, but after a couple of years of married life she lost interest in sex. Any congress of that nature was reduced to a grudging and minimalist effort, always hurried as if there were more urgent things waiting to be done. 'Are you finished yet?' she would say, staring at the stipples on the ceiling and I would look at the label sticking up on her nightdress and think it the most unsexy thing ever invented.

I never cheated on Myrtle (except perhaps in my mind – maybe I'm cheating now), but we were growing even more estranged as the years rolled by. Makes you think of the whole idea of monogamy. For better or for worse, that sort of thing. I often walk by the canal and stand on the old bridge and watch the swans. However, I never saw them pecking at each other the way Myrtle pecks at me. But even they have gone now, ever since the cider-drinkers arrived (they used to stone them). One went first. I didn't see her go but I saw the second one leaving. He (I'm just guessing it was the cob) suddenly raised his heavy wings one day as if they had come from a secret part of himself and, flapping ponderously, tore down the canal like a plane on a runway, his legs skimming along the surface of the water until airborne. Then, wavering for a moment, like someone remembering, he lifted himself higher and flew away.

It's Tuesday night and Sandra is bopping. My window is open. I hear the rustling of feet on leaves and the crunching of a snail shell and I think of my father saying that if you went close enough to a snail you could hear it cry (that's when my dad could hear). The sound comes from the garden next to mine. I can't see anyone because of its high wall and the falling darkness. A light from a window makes a tall conifer throw out a shadow, and it is from that shadow I see the glow of a cigarette getting brighter as it is deeply inhaled.

My curiosity gets the better of me and I risk asking Myrtle if Ida ever mentioned anything about the people in the houses around the back.

She gives me one of her looks. 'Ida,' she says, 'since when is it Ida and not the old wag?' What do you want to know them for?'

'No, it's just that a ball landed in our back garden. I was wondering did it belong to them.'

I knew it didn't belong to them. I knew it belonged to the kid, Freddy, next door. I've seen him play with it on the avenue, a white ball with black diamond-shaped marks.

'It's those brats on the avenue. They'll break a window soon. I'll burst their ball on them.'

'I was just curious,' I say. 'It was only for the sake of a bit of conversation.'

'You're showing your true colours now,' she says, 'you're just as interested in gossip as the people you down.'

I'm walking along the road which leads into the avenue on my way home from work. A squirrel rushes up one of the chestnut trees that line the road, getting supplies in for winter no doubt, just like us on the avenue stocking up on our oil and coal and thermal underwear.

'Hiya, Franky.' The voice comes from high up in one of the trees. I look up and see Freddy Browne near the top.

'Be careful up there,' I say

'We're collecting conkers, Franky,' he shouts. I hate that first name business from a kid of his age. He never calls me Mr Copeland.

'Hiya, Franky,' says another voice, and then I see a boy with a pudgy face lurking lower down the tree. Freddy has a stick, and I hold my breath as he stretches and strikes a branch, and a spiked green bur like the miniature head of a knight's mace falls in a shower of leaves.

'That's a big one, Freddy,' shouts the pudgy-faced boy.

I come home to discover that Myrtle is out. With my mind on Sandra, I go into the back garden and take the football which I had seen earlier from under the privet. I put it into a plastic bag so that the kid, Freddy Browne won't see it if I pass him on the avenue. Myrtle gave out to his parents about their kid. She butted in. 'What business is it of yours?' I said and she looked at me suspiciously for a moment and went out the door harping on about how they should mind the kid more and not let him roam the streets for half the night. She came back in an awful state. That George fellow, the father, told her to fuck off. 'Some father,' she said, 'he doesn't deserve the title.'

I lock the front door of the house and walk down the avenue. It's dusky. Smoke is snaking out of some chimneys. I feel it catching in my lungs. In the distance I hear, sporadically, the premature explosions of Halloween bangers, unnerving, sending sudden jolts to the heart. Kids don't think of the heart, of the trembling of old folk behind doors, watching at windows, listening at letterboxes, like frightened animals in pens.

The trees on the verges stand out under the veiled light of the street lamps. Those which have been vandalised are denuded already, while the leaves continue to spiral down in ones and twos from their more fortunate comrades. Funny that, the colder it gets the more the trees shed.

I hear and then see Freddy Browne standing under a street lamp with his dog. He's a small kid about ten or eleven, orphan-thin with a strident voice – you'll always hear Freddy's voice above that of others (except for Myrtle's of course). His facial skin is pinkblotched, and brown curls protrude through a baseball cap which he wears back-to-front. He's holding a big glass jar out of which he is distributing sweets to a group of kids who are circled around him. The dog jumps up on Freddy.

'Wait your turn, Melancholy,' Freddy shouts.

He looks up and sees me.

'Hiya, Franky.'

'Hiya,' I say resigning myself to familiarity.

'Fancy a cough sweet, Franky?'

'No. I'll wait till I get a cough.'

The kids laugh.

'That's a good one, Franky.'

'They last for ages.'

'That's only if you suck them slow.'

'Where did you get the jar?' I say.

'Found it,' Freddy says with a roguish grin.

The sole of Freddy's left boot has come unstuck and flaps as he moves around. There's a hole punched in its side like what they do with charity footwear so it can't be pawned.

'Yeah. Freddy found it,' says the pudgy-faced boy.

'What's your name?' I say.

'John Paul.'

I see a couple of smaller kids down the avenue playing conkers.

'What did you do with the chestnuts?' I say.

'Sold them,' says John Paul.

'Don't mind him, Franky,' says Freddy. 'We gave them away. That's kid's stuff. We just wanted to climb the trees.'

'You like climbing?' I say.

'Yeah,' says John Paul.

'You didn't by any chance see me ball in your garden, Franky?'

11

Freddy says.

'Ball?' I say, clutching the plastic bag tightly in my hand.

'Yeah. A black and white one. It went in before. Could I go in and have a look? I do be afraid to go in when she's there.'

'She?'

'The Ballcutter. She'd cut me up. Me oul fella told me to have nothing to do with her.'

I remember Myrtle putting a knife through one of their footballs when she said it broke a branch off our Robinia. But I never saw any sign of a broken branch. 'Where's the branch?' I said to her. 'What do you mean? In the yellow tree.' Myrtle hasn't a clue about the names of trees. 'Where?' I said, looking out at the tree, 'there's no break.' 'There you go again, just trying to get my back up.' The kids gathered outside the garden after it happened as if they were holding a postmortem on the ball, holding the deflated piece of plastic up in the air on a stick. They chanted outside the house, 'Ballcutter, Ballcutter,' until it got dark.

I could have said you shouldn't call my wife that name. I could have told them but I didn't.

'I know she's your missus, Franky,' Freddy says, realising the awkwardness of the situation, 'but I hate her.'

'And she's hairy,' says a skinny kid with a tight stepped haircut called Tomo.

Myrtle has an incipient moustache, gradually thickening with the years. She doesn't shave it. The hair started out of a mole on the left side of her upper lip.

'Maybe she's a man,' says a plump young one whom I recognise as the girl with the doll.

'Shut up, Sue Ellen.'

'No. I won't shut up.'

'No,' I say, 'there's no ball. I would have seen it if it were in my garden.'

'Freddy gave it a massive kick,' John Paul says admiringly, 'it went so high it could have landed in the houses at the back.'

I try to imagine running to kick a ball with your sole flapping in one boot.

Freddy's eyes light up at the other kid's compliment. 'It was a fuckin' good kick all right, I'll say, Franky.'

I'll say, Franky. The little runt is trying to sound older than his years. He's talking as if he's my adult peer. They don't understand, these kids, what youth is until they've left it behind.

'If I see any sign of it I'll drop it over your wall,' I say, trying to ignore the kids' bad language. I mean do they have to say *fuckin'* at their age? They all use it now. I suppose it's a form of punctuation; it doesn't really mean what it means.

'Come in, it's late, Sue Ellen,' a mother calls. The name doesn't quite trip the same on a Dublin guttural as it does on a Dallas drawl.

Freddy's legs are dangling on the wall, emphasising the flapping sole. Impetuously I say, 'Your boots, can you get them mended?'

'The oul fella, he wouldn't ...'

'Here,' I offer Freddy a twenty note. I've no smaller change. What the hell. I feel sorry for the kid. Besides I'm borrowing his ball. 'That'll go towards a new pair.'

He looks at me suspiciously.

'What do I have to do for that?' he says

'What do you mean? You don't have to do anything.'

'You mean it?'

'Of course I mean it.'

His eyes brighten. 'Thanks, Franky.'

He runs off towards the green space near the pylon, summoning all the kids, shouting, 'Look what Franky gave me.'

As I walk on down the avenue I hear the sound of bolts. Barricades are lifted; a door opens and old Mr what'shisname comes out of his fortress, unshaven and dazed, gone to pieces since his wife died.

'It's staying dry,' I say, annoyed that I can't think of his real name.

He mooches towards me and rests a hand on my sleeve.

13

'Come 'ere,' he says, 'what day is it?'

'Monday,' I say.

'Monday?' he says, reflecting for a moment, and then returns to his house muttering something to himself.

I walk on and around the corner towards the houses at the back.

I know Sandra's house (I've really convinced myself she's Sandra) because directly opposite through the gable end gap I can see the yellow privet jutting up over my shed, and higher up I see my study window, dark and lifeless now. Sandra's garden is shadowed by a cypress tree grown scraggly and out of proportion to the small space allotted to it. I take the ball out of the bag and crumple the plastic into my jacket pocket. There's a rectangular sign saying *Blue Moon* hanging by two chains from the ceiling of the porch. I straighten my tie, run my fingers through my hair trying in vain to see myself through the glass in the porch which is lighted from the landing inside, and I feel my heart give a little flutter before my finger presses the bell.

There is no answer. I'm inclined to walk away, to flee perhaps – I mean the whole idea is preposterous – and then the door opens. A middle-aged woman appears in heavy makeup, bottle-blonde, her hair not unlike Ida's (maybe Ida did her hair). She is more fleshy than Ida though, especially her upper arms which she reveals through a short-sleeved blouse.

'What can I do for you, lurve?' she says in an English accent.

'The ball,' I say, 'I was wondering ... was it yours?'

It's an absurd question. Even my imagination would not stretch far enough to see this overweight old dear as the owner of a football.

'The ball?' she says, looking alarmed, 'are you a detective?'

'Of course not. It's just I found it in my garden. I thought that maybe one of your children or...'

She takes the ball from me and examines it.

'Seamless.'

'What?'

'The way some of them are made.'

She hands the ball back with a smile. 'I have no children, lurve. Just a girl and she's grown up.'

'Sorry, it must belong to some other house. You see my house is...'

'Sorry, lurve.'

'Sorry for troubling you.'

'Ta ra, lurve.'

As I make my way towards the gate the old dear shouts after me, 'Call anytime, anytime you feel like it, lurve. Just ask for Dorothy.'

'Thank you.'

'And you don't need to bring your big ball either.'

She bursts out laughing. I feel foolish, embarrassed as I walk away with her laughter ringing in my ears, and with a ball which seems to have grown to an enormous size sticking out from under my oxter.

As I go out the gate I see George Browne coming towards me. He must have spotted me, because he suddenly turns around and walks back the way he had come.

It's Sunday and I'm on my way to Mass. I go to Mass the odd time, not as much as I used to, mind; maybe it's to do with my inability to kneel or maybe it's more to do with watching Myrtle strutting down the avenue linked to her friend Ida every Sunday morning for the ten o'clock Mass. I mean if they're going to heaven then maybe I'd rather go to the other place, if other place there is. It's a couple of months since I went last – a couple of months, God I'm beginning to sound guilty already like I'm in a confessional. *How long is it now since... my son?*

When I go in the door Mrs Dempsey's singing priest is emerging from the sacristy followed by his two altar boys, pristine in their surpluses and soutanes. Mrs Dempsey herself is already standing in her lopsided way in the front pew with her missal open before the rest of the congregation have risen. I often try to guess her age. She must be as old as my father, but her mind is sharp and clear. She is a woman who, apart from a bad hip, wears her mortality well. She could pass for any age from sixty upwards, a woman who has reached a stasis, who can't get fatter or thinner or older, who will remain the same until she just fades away. She lives in one of the old cottages near my father. She was chasing priests even before her husband died. Many's the party she had in her cottage – my father and I were often invited. This ageing priest she is particularly fond of – Father Mack – is on the altar now. His real name is Father McEnroe but everyone calls him Father Mack. He used to sing the same song at Mrs Dempsey's parties in seven different languages. I remember it was so boring (even the name of the song escapes me), but we had to sit through the seven versions, my father and I, and applaud at the end. 'Wasn't he wonderful?' Mrs Dempsey would say and my father, twirling a corner of his moustache, would reply, 'Wonderful is not the word, Philomena', and I never found out if he was being sarcastic or not. And I remember the priest's cheeks glowing from the adulation, or else it was from the whiskey with which Mrs Dempsey was generously plying him. And she had the priest around to her cottage not only for singing but also for social calls and for advice-to-widow calls after her husband died, and on Sundays he called for 'a bit of roast'. And I began to think that Mrs Dempsey latched onto a priest in the hope of getting a plenary indulgence for the afterlife. Or maybe it was her way of seeking a life suture, stitching herself warmly within sacerdotal folds. Her clinging to a priest was like my clinging to a book or my father's clinging to the Diamond public house. She keeps active in the parish despite her advancing years. She still provides the flowers for the church altar, mostly from her cottage garden, and occasionally, if she is short, from my father's, although a lot of the flowers are bought now.

Father Mack is tall, although a bit stooped now and nearly completely bald. Does he still have the spotless fingernails that I remember for giving out the Host? (So clean compared to my father's under which there normally resides a permanent sediment of soil). And through the vestments the ventricose belly, protruding no doubt from all the roast dinners that Mrs Dempsey has been feeding him.

Freddy Browne is standing near me in the same pew picking his nose. He is intent on picking it, drilling deep inside with his forefinger trying to dislodge some stubborn snot, apparently lost or indifferent to his surroundings when the priest says, 'Let us offer each other the sign of peace,' and Freddy, suddenly focusing, takes his finger out of his nose and offers me his hand to shake saying, 'Peace be with ya, Franky.'

Freddy is like some plant gradually shooting up out of the dark sward of my consciousness. His parents, George and Noreen I hardly see at all. Myrtle calls Freddy a brat. 'Why do you call him a brat?' I say when I return home after Mass. 'Who?' she says. 'Freddy Browne. He doesn't strike me as a brat.'

She stops drying a cup which she was attacking as if she was taking the core out of an apple. 'It just goes to show how much you know,' she says, 'and that dog of theirs keeps the whole avenue awake at night.' 'I'm going to complain. Selfish people,' she says, 'dogs are not made for suburban estates.'

I can't argue with Myrtle about the noise of their dog.

'He's never home,' Myrtle says, 'that's why the brat runs wild.'

'Who's never home?'

'His father, that George fella.'

The evening is closing in on the front garden and I'm unenthusiastically sweeping up leaves when Myrtle comes out ready for her visit to Ida. She's wearing her vixen-red lipstick and is reeking of perfume. Once in a while I'm tempted to ask her if she'd like to go to the cinema again with me like we used to on Sunday evenings in the early days. I did ask in fact a couple of times but it's the same answer, the same rhetorical question as I get in the matrimonial bed.

Freddy Browne is sitting on his garden wall, his dog nearby. Myrtle walks past him and then turns back, takes a paper handkerchief out of her handbag and offers it to him.

'Wipe your nose,' she says.

'I don't want that.'

The dog sniffs at her feet. She shoos him away.

'Of course not. You'd rather go around snotty-nosed. Does your mother look after you at all?'

'Me mother is an invalid.'

'And what about your father, is he an invalid too?'

Freddy doesn't answer. Doesn't get a chance. It's more a parting shot from Myrtle as she walks on. Myrtle is good at parting shots.

Tomo and John Paul run across from the green where they were playing to join Freddy. They watch until Myrtle has gone down near the end of the avenue before they shout, 'Ballcutter, Ballcutter,' but Myrtle doesn't turn around.

Sandra is becoming more demonstrative. This Tuesday she is gesturing to me. She delineates her curvature with her hands going down her body like a river over rocks and through eddies. Why do I say that? There are no rocks or eddies. Too much reading. But Sandra's hands are not just hands; they are a language that moves like Myrtle's tongue. She is beckoning me now with her hands, her fingers bending towards her, her thumbs remaining upright like little pillars through which I am invited to pass. She pouts and puckers in an attempt to imitate a sophistication. The sophistication of glamour girls in glossy magazines and Hollywood films. Her lips are moving. *Come on over.* She turns and takes up different poses, looks sideways at the lighted window, then curls her left index finger to draw me in.

Maybe she has been repressed in some way. Appearing in the lighted window is an act of rebellion, a declaration of independence. Maybe she has met her first boyfriend, has sampled her first sexual fumbling. She wants to impress him with her newly acquired knowledge. But maybe there is no boyfriend. She does it all for me. She must see me. How could she see me? There is no light in the room where I stand. I turn my gaze towards the neighbouring garden. I see the flame on the cigarette getting brighter.

Myrtle is at the vanity mirror brushing her hair with her bone-handled brush, her silk dressing gown hanging loose. Her hair, despite the passing of the years, still holds its lustre. She brushes. How many strokes? Slowly, sensuously. She catches my eye in the mirror. 'What are you looking at?' she says accusingly. 'Nothing,' I say. 'Why aren't you stuck in your book?' 'Are you coming to bed?' I say, turned on, feeling a warmth after Sandra. 'When I'm ready,' she says curtly.

'What is wrong with you these days? You keep at me.' Myrtle says in bed as she rebuffs another of my physical advances. 'What devil has got into you?'

I turn on my side away from her and sigh. Another night the same. How many? Never counted before. I hear Browne's dog barking. He's baying at the moon as Halloween approaches. Baying and baying until the moon in desperation gives way to the early light.

Sandra has set me thinking, pondering on my marriage. Where did it all begin? Where did it all go wrong? I was only nineteen when I married Myrtle. Young and naive yes, but determined to do the honourable thing, reconciling myself at the time to what I thought was going to be my role as a husband and father of a child. Despite my youth, I took my responsibilities seriously; years of caring for my own father had ensured that. I could have waited perhaps, delayed a little, bided my time, checked out the menu as they say. The sweet taste of hindsight. But Myrtle didn't want to wait. What would people think if she was going around with a bump, she said, and no husband to call her own? Ah yes, the bump. What would people think indeed?

She was quite a few years older than me – seven to be precise – and she knew it was the right thing to do. She was alluring then and very mature I thought, not like some of the flirtatious young ones who used to hang around the avenue who were just teases and ran away if you tried anything. But Myrtle was experienced. I never enquired how or where she got the experience. I was too busy being happy.

But I gradually noticed there was no change in her, apart from the physical change that is. There was none of this maternal excitement about having a baby, no expectations, no buying of cots or prams or preparation of baby rooms, no stuff like that. I put it down to the kid being conceived before marriage and to a desire to do things quietly, but now I don't know. I didn't know then for example that she hated children.

She hated Ivy Cottage where we were to live with my father. She couldn't live there. She hated my father. His depressing ways. She was going over to Ida's. 'You can't do that,' I said. 'You can't just walk out.' But she did. She stopped seeing me for several months.

I remember calling to Ida's place, a one bedroom apartment by the canal. I demanded to see my wife but I was shooed away by Ida. 'Have you got the money?' she said. 'What money?' 'For the down payment on a house?' She looked at me with a malevolent grin. 'The baby?' I said. 'It's not due for a while,' she said. 'Be patient.' 'Who are you to tell me what to do? I want to talk to my wife.' She sighed. 'Look, I'm just delivering a message. She's not well. She can't come to see you. She needs a woman to take care of her, in the condition she's in, you understand?' I tried to push in past her. She held the door firmly. 'You're trespassing,' she said.

A woman to take care of her, in the condition she's in. I was naive enough to believe that. I was sure I would see Myrtle at the shop or at Mass or walking down the avenue. But there was no sign. She had disappeared. Was she out of the country? Was she lying low in Ida's place all that time? I was too embarrassed to ask anyone where my own wife was. Few people said anything. My dad was away in his own world, and Mrs Dempsey would look up to heaven any time Myrtle's name was mentioned.

I saved for several months. I borrowed from Dad. I took some money out of his savings. I asked him of course if it was all right. He nodded. I hoped he understood. I called back to Ida's. I knocked at her door. They refused to answer. I shouted in the letter box. 'Tell her I have the money for the down payment.'

The next day she sent Ida over to say I had the 'all clear' to see her again. I was to be kind and gentle to her because it was a terrible experience for a woman to have a miscarriage. But when I looked at Ida's pushed-in nose, all I could think of was a boxer.

When I went over 'to collect' Myrtle, the door was ajar (they

21

were expecting me) and she was sitting beside Ida on a settee in front of a two-pronged electric fire. They were joking and laughing at one of Ida's anti-male blue jokes, about cutting some guy's balls off, if I remember correctly. Ida was always talking about cutting something or other. Maybe it was because she was a hairdresser, I really don't know, but she always carried a scissors in her handbag. And she was able to use language forthrightly long before the arrival of what my father called 'women's lip'.

They were eating potato crisps and drinking bottles of Guinness. They could have been a bit drunk, I don't know, but I'll always remember the look they gave me when I came in. It was the weirdest look, almost like non-recognition, like it was saying, *Who are you, stranger*? And then Ida announced sarcastically, 'Your whosebinned is here,' and they both burst into a titter.

But I remember, despite all that, being still hopeful at the time and saying to myself I'd ride out this storm, if storm it was, and I prayed that such behaviour was just a little hiccup at the beginning of a marriage, and that with patience it would resolve itself in time.

I don't know what Sandra has done to me, subliminally of course. She has activated some cerebral switch and turned on some memory channel formerly defunct. These days in the manor library where I work, when I have a spare moment, instead of the usual novel browsing, I find myself looking up books and encyclopaedias on miscarriage. They all say that women can become depressed or emotionally upset from having one, and that it can take a long time (if ever) to get over it.

I'm reading the local paper when Myrtle is clearing away plates after the evening meal. 'A woman abandoned her child,' I read out loud, 'at the garda station. Could you believe that? Just left it there and then fled into the night before anyone could find out anything about her.'

'Heartless,' says Myrtle.

'The only thing that's known about her is that she had a mop of wild black hair.'

'Who?'

'The woman.'

'Probably a wig. And what's going to happen to the child?'

'It's in the hospital at the moment, but if no one comes to claim it soon, it will be put up for adoption.'

Myrtle takes up a plate she already had dried.

'How could anyone abandon a child?' I say.

She doesn't answer.

'I'm speaking to you,' I say.

'I've got things to do.'

'Do you ever hear anything I say?'

'Don't you start.'

'The foetus, what did you ever do with it?'

'What are you talking about? What foetus?'

'The miscarriage?'

'That was years ago.'

'What did you do with it?'

She bangs the plates loudly. 'What did I do with it? What do you mean what did I do with it? Ida got rid of it.'

'Got rid of it, her?'

'Why are you asking all this now, resurrecting the past?'

'It didn't bother you, did it?'

'What would you know what bothered me?'

'How many months was it?'

'How many months? What are you on about?'

'It had a soul, Myrtle.'

'You're trying to upset me. Something's eating you lately. Who have you been talking to?'

'We should've baptised it.'

'Now you've done it,' she screams, and she storms out of the room.

I go outside for a while to let the cool of the evening calm me. I do that a lot when Myrtle goes on the rampage. I'm used to her by now knocking doors off hinges. Nothing new there.

I walk down the garden path kicking a used starlight into the border shrubbery. Halloween has come and gone apparently without major incident according to the newspaper. A few fires. A few fire brigades followed by the usual debris cleanup of cider flagons and burnt-out fireworks.

I see George Browne outside his house, a cigarette in the corner of his mouth, sweeping up leaves that have blown into his tarmac garden (George has no time for lawns; besides, his white van takes up most of the garden space). He's tall and dapper looking – a ringer for Errol Flynn minus the twinkle – with oiled hair (a few matted strands cascade over his right eye) and neatly trimmed moustache without the slightest touch of grey. Dapper looking that is, once you don't look down at his Doc Martens. They must be at least size thirteen. I go over to him carrying the football which I'd left in the front garden

24

under the laurel hedge.

'Hello, George,' I say.

He crushes his cigarette under a boot and toes it into a little cluster of used bangers, half hidden among the leaves.

'I wish they'd all fall at the one time and get done with it,' he says. 'I just swept them up two days ago.'

Often when you look at someone you see that one eye looks kinder than another, as if there are two halves to a person, a hard and a soft part. But both of George's eyes look hard.

'The ball,' I say.

'That's Freddy's. I'll give it to him.'

George takes the ball and throws it into his porch. It's all right, George I say to myself, you don't have to waste time with sissy words like thanks, a big man like you.

'How is Freddy, George?' I say.

'Fine.'

'And Noreen?' I ask quietly, conscious of a new social role, but afraid of overdoing it.

He gives me a look for a moment, a bit like one of Myrtle's suspicious looks.

'She's fine too... whenever I see her.'

'You travel a lot?'

I'm overdoing the questions. I'm worse than Myrtle now.

'On and off.'

'What do you sell George?'

'What's this, twenty questions?'

'Sorry.'

'Condom machines. I don't sell them. I install them. And what do you sell?'

'Books. I don't sell them. I lend them.'

'Don't have time for books,' George says. His tone has changed, become sullen. He turns away, resumes his sweeping, dismisses me with, 'I better get these up before the rain comes.'

Myrtle is whistling when I return to the house. She whistles quite often. At first I used to think she whistled because she couldn't sing, in other words it was her way of expressing her feelings, her humours. It was only later I realised her whistling was a political act. She whistles, not to express, but to hide a humour or a secret, or to drown out things she doesn't want to hear, especially from me. She is busy in the kitchen. The kitchen is Myrtle's kingdom. She hangs pots and plates and cutlery on walls like art exhibits (Doors don't figure). I walk around her gingerly to get the teapot.

'I haven't heard the dog bark these last few nights,' I say, trying to break the irritating sound, and at the same time trying to steer clear of confrontation (the matter of the miscarriage has been let lie).

She stops whistling. A victory.

'They must've impounded him.'

'I haven't seen Noreen around.'

'Since when have you ever seen Noreen around?'

'George said she was fine.'

'Ha. He would, wouldn't he?'

'What do you mean?'

'Ida says she has a broken rib cage after he knocked her down.'

'Knocked her down?'

'Something's going to happen there, something worse, one of these days, mark my words.'

Myrtle's words trail off like smoke as she leaves the room. She thrives on the excitement of hearsay; it energises her and she goes off whistling and hoovering at a fierce rate.

Freddy is playing with his own ball again. He is playing football with a group of boys on the green near the pylon. Freddy is quite skilful with a ball; he tackles well, he has fast feet despite the flapping boot; the other boys find it difficult to win the ball from him. 'Pass it, pass it,' and 'over here,' some of them shout through the dusk, but Freddy is singleminded, determined as he progresses up the green on a solo run, outfoxes the defence and scores a goal. A cry goes up from his team, and John Paul shouts, 'A fuckin' massive kick.'

Hard to see now as darkness falls, but the kids, with eyes like cats, play on undeterred by the world's transformations.

I sit on the garden wall under the light of a street lamp as the game fizzles out, darkness the ultimate victor.

'Hiya, Franky,' says Freddy, coming to sit on the wall beside me. His voice is subdued, lacking its usual chirpiness. John Paul and Tomo join us. A gust blows up.

'It's raining leaves, Franky,' says John Paul.

Freddy has a big bruise over his left eye.

'Where did you get the shiner?' I say.

'Ah, it's nothin'.'

Freddy says no more, making it clear that he doesn't want to explain anything.

'Fancy a mint?' I say.

'Are they the ones with the hole?'

'No,' I say, 'they're bad value.'

'Thanks, Franky.'

'Thanks, Franky.'

More kids approach and I'm soon cleaned out of sweets.

'It's a nice evenin', Franky.'

I'm getting used to adult-speak, with kids that is. John Paul is right. The evening is nice, nice and dry, no wind (except for that odd gust), no frost, mild enough to sit outside on a garden wall.

John Paul nudges Tomo. 'Go on tell him.'

Tomo hesitates.

'Go on.'

'We saw the English one.'

'What?'

'We saw her changin'.'

'Through the window.'

'We got a good decko from Freddy's garden.'

'We saw her diddies.'

For a moment I think they are testing me, that they know I've seen her too, and yet the tone is boastful, non-accusatory.

'Your dog,' I say, trying to change the subject, 'I don't hear him bark anymore.'

There is an immediate lull. The kids look at Freddy. Freddy lowers his head.

'You don't know the story?'

'No.'

'Tell him, Freddy.'

'Yeah,' shouts a chorus.

Freddy takes a butt of a cigarette and a match out of his trouser pocket He checks behind that no one is at his window, then strikes the match off the wall and, like an experienced smoker, cups his hand around the flame until he is puffing smoke.

'Do you not think you're a bit...?'

'It calms me down.'

Calms him down. Sounds like a grown-up neurotic.

Freddy wets the tip of his finger and applies it to the side of the butt which is not burning evenly.

I suck on my mint.

'Why are you always eating mints, Franky?' asks John Paul.

'It keeps me off those things,' I say, pointing to Freddy's stabber.

'I feck them from me oul fella, from his breast pocket,' Freddy says. 'He never misses them. He comes in so pissed he doesn't notice anythin".

'Tell him what else you found,' says John Paul.

Freddy hesitates.

'Go on.'

'You wont squeal?'

'No,' I say.

I don't know why they're taking me into their confidence. Maybe they don't see me in the typical authoritarian light of an adult world. Maybe they can trace a lost childhood somewhere in my face.

'He found a used johnny with the stabbers. Didn't you, Freddy?'

'Yeah.'

'Where is your da now?' I say.

'He's fucked off on us.'

'Will he be back?'

'Who knows? Who cares?'

'You were going to tell me about your dog.'

'Maybe another time.'

'Tell him,' says John Paul.

'Go on,' says Tomo.

'That dog was almost a purebred, what do they call it?'

'He had pedigree,' I say.

'Yeah,' says Freddy, 'a cocker spaniel, but when I said that me oul fella said, "Cocker spaniel me arse; he's half a cocker and half a conger eel". He was a bit lame but he could still play with me.'

'And with me too,' says John Paul

'He played with all of us,' says Tomo.

'Me ma says he was lame because he was probably thrun out of a car after Christmas.'

He looks around, inhales deeply. 'Anyways we're goin' down to the field by the canal. Melancholy's sniffin' about.'

'How did he get the name?' I say.

'Me oul fella christened him. "Fuckin' melancholy," that's

what he said when he saw him. You know the way their eyes are, on cocker spaniels I mean, like they're always cryin'?' Anyways,' he continues, 'we're down by the canal, Melancholy and me hidin' behind a bush, lookin' at the cider-drinkers standin' around a fire, when it happens.'

'What happens?' I say

'Wait for it,' says John Paul.

'Give us another mint, Franky.'

'He's none left.'

'A hand,' says Tomo.

'Let Freddy tell it,' says John Paul.

'I feel this hand tight on me mouth and I'm wheeled around to face a scumbag who blows smoke into me face. And he lifts up me hand.'

'His left hand,' says John Paul

'He lifts up me left hand and presses his cigarette into it.'

'The lit cigarette.'

'Like it was an ashtray,' says Tomo.

'"Squeal," he says, 'but I don't make a sound.'

'Show him,' says John Paul. 'Show him the mark on your hand.'

Freddy shows me the burn in the centre of his left palm.

'"Somethin' stronger," says he when I make no sound, and he takes out a blade real shiny.'

'Ooooh,' say the audience.

'Melancholy jumps up on him and tears a piece out of his hand, and the scumbag runs off down to the canal, cursin' and screamin'. " I'll get you, Freddy Browne," he shouts. "I'll get you and your fuckin' dog. Wait and see.'"

'That was Spikey,' says Tomo. 'Spikey always produces the blade.'

'Tomo knows about the cider-drinkers,' says Freddy. 'His brother's one of them.'

'Not any more,' says Tomo.

'No, not anymore,' says Freddy

'No fuckin' way.'

'They're going to get him,' says John Paul.

'No, they're not,' says Tomo.

'Yes, they are. They're goin' to get him for rattin'.'

Freddy glances behind him.

'You're ma's not lookin',' says Tomo.

'His ma thinks he's a delinquent,' says John Paul.

'Why does she think that?'

'Because he goes off sometimes.'

'Is that true?'

'He sells things as well.'

'Sells things?'

'Yeah. He sells batteries at half price if you ever want them.'

'For Walkmans,' says Tomo.

'Not just them. Other stuff as well,' says Freddy.

'Get on with the story,' says Tomo. 'I'll be called in soon.'

'We hear bangers explodin'. Melancholy doesn't like the bangers; they frighten him, see, and he sort of makes a little cry every time one explodes. So I takes him home.'

'Your ma gave us some stuff, 'says John Paul.

'Yeah, and then we all scarper down to the canal to watch the bonfires. We're lookin' at these for a while when Melancholy sidles up to me out of the blue. I point towards the house. I'm cross with him for getting out and he knows it; he puts his head down, whines a bit and limps away.'

'They were gettin' high on jungle juice,' says John Paul.

'They're bleedin' fireworks were rapeh,' says Tomo, 'so we leg it down to get a better look.'

'We smell the rubber of the car tyres burnin'.'

'Then we notice it.'

'Notice what?' I say.

'They take a dog out of a sack,' says Tomo. 'His mouth all taped up.'

I look at Freddy. He has gone silent. He is breathing heavily. Tears are welling.

'Flames are jumpin', hands are wavin' like in a dance.'

'Tell him what you feel, Freddy.'

'I feel the heat of the fire burnin' into me and I can taste the vomit risin.'

'The dog's legs are tied,' says John Paul.

Freddy takes an inhaler out of his pocket. Sucks frantically. 'Kick out, Melancholy,' he cries. 'Kick out. Jesus will come.'

Myrtle wants new wallpaper in our bedroom. Ida, she says, saw some nice wallpaper down in the Centre.

I saw nothing wrong with the old wallpaper; there wasn't a mark on it but I never liked the design: huge orange tulips. I mean I never saw orange tulips.

We're sitting having breakfast. Or I'm sitting. She's flitting about or hovering intermittently in some space between cooker and dresser. Her floral apron on, she's taking out eggs and flour and sugar preparing for a baking day, another fancy cake for her friend Ida. Does Ida eat cake? To look at her Spartan self, one would have to say no – one surmises Ida devouring jungle berries and raw flesh.

'What's that noise?' I say to Myrtle, putting my cup down, suddenly hearing the sound of a chainsaw outside the house.

'They're cutting down the trees on the road,' she says.

'What? The Chestnuts?'

'Whatever you call them.'

'Why?'

'*Why*, he says, will you listen to him?' She turns her back on me and starts furiously whipping eggs and sugar into a froth. 'They were all diseased, that's why.'

'They were not,' I say.

'Even the Council said they were too old, and besides, they were scratching the bus.'

'They were not scratching the bus.'

'The Council said they were a danger.'

'A danger?'

'They could've fallen on top of us.'

'So that's it,' I say.

'I'm going to strip the walls,' she says, 'after I do the cake.'

33

'What cake is it this time?'

'What's it look like. Angel cake, do you mind?'

I put on my coat and, as I'm going out the door for work, she shouts, 'Don't forget to collect the wallpaper on your way home. It's paid for. All you have to do is collect it.'

Hard to hear the sound of the traffic with the chainsaws going at full throttle across the road. I'm at the head of a long queue for the eight thirty bus. I normally walk to work. The library is less than a mile away but today it's raining, a persistent drizzle, getting heavier.

I see George Browne at the tail end of the queue. I wave to him. One of the black students, with teeth as white and uniform as piano ivory and a sparkling white shirt to match, is standing beside him. George gives a token nod as he exhales from his cigarette. The first of the day? He looks dishevelled, hungover. Where did he spend the night? And Noreen? Did she sob all night long? It was none of my business.

'Could I touch you for the price of the fare?' George says, coming up to me.

'Eh you, get back in your place,' a man with a lunch box shouts.

'We were here first,' says a woman with a brolly, who looks like she's ready to hit George with it.

'Hey man,' shouts the black student.

I give George the money.

'Keep your knickers on,' George shouts at the protesters, 'I'm going back.'

George sits beside me on the top deck.

'Thanks, Franky,' he says, his first time to address me by name, but who gave him the right to cull the shorter version of me, a right he has obviously handed down to his son? 'I'll give it back to you later,' he says. 'I was in such a rush this morning.'

'Where's your van?'

'That's where I'm going now.'

'A service?'

George wrinkles his forehead in a worried frown. 'They

knocked off me wheels.'

'Who?'

'Who do you think?'

'The cider-drinkers?'

'They wanted the tires for their fucking bonfires.'

The bus screeches to a stop, picks up more people, only standing room, 'Have you been down to the Diamond lately?' George says.

'No.'

'You should go down. I was down there the other evening fitting a condom machine.'

'I thought they had a condom machine.'

'This was in the *Ladies*.'

'The *Ladies*?'

'Yeah, they buy more than the men. But anyway I heard them saying they were bringing in strippers.'

The word brings wallpaper into my mind. 'Strippers, you say?'

'Yeah, pubs will do anything to boost their sales.'

I open the library book to stamp its return date. Its leaves have kept intact a strong smell of crisps. Amazing what's found in library books: lollipop sticks, bills, tickets for buses or cinema or disco or even lottery tickets and not all of them used, cigarette burns, egg or coffee or wine or chocolate stains, pages stuck together with chewing gum, dog ears, phrases underlined with pencil or ink, margins annotated, or for those less diligent whole pages ripped out, letters of personal or political indignation (rarely of praise) written under the title page of the book. Games: if you want to know who I am turn to page x column y first letter of ninth word is the last letter of my second Christian name, then proceed to... or other notes decrying the vandalised state of the book, apparently not realising that their words are also defacing the book. Perhaps a blank page should be inserted in all books like the blackboard for graffiti on the new buses. But the blackboard is always bare. There is no fun in that. It has to be furtive.

I stamp its first date on a new book. I love reading a book new. I'm addicted to its smell like ovenfresh bread or the smell of plastic in a new car (one of the few things about a car I like). Renewals are busy today, interrupting my reading or rather my rereading of *Gulliver's Travels*. It's like I'm retracing things. Where was I? Oh yes, Gulliver was hanging out of some giant woman's nipple. Don't remember that bit. I suppose you read the same book with different eyes when you're older.

I look out the window onto the street. I see Freddy slingeing along, hands in his pockets kicking a can, John Paul following further back. They're probably mitching from school. Can't blame Freddy for being unsettled after what happened to his dog. I open the window of the library and shout to him to coax him in. The library is officially closed for lunch so there is no one around except for Michael Troy, the library assistant, and he's probably off somewhere looking up facts. He's big into facts is Michael.

'Hiya, Franky,' Freddy says nervously throwing his head in the door. You can sense the desolation in his voice. A deep world-weary sigh.

'Come on in, come on in,' I say. 'What's new?'

'Nothin''

The pockets of his short pants are loaded with something. He looks cursorily around at all the books.

'You're interested in stories, aren't you?' I say trying to enthuse him.

'True ones,' he says with a yawn.

'Did you sleep last night?' I say.

'What's it to you?' he says.

'It's just you look tired.'

'I better go,' he says.

'You can read about true stories too.' I lead him along the shelves. He slouches after me dragging his feet reluctantly as if they were heavy weights.

'Here,' I say. I pick a book. '*The Adventures of Alexander Selkirk,* that's a true story.' I put the book into his hands. 'You've heard of Robinson Crusoe?'

'I don't want to *read* about things. I want to do things.'

He hands the book back to me. 'Sorry, Franky.'

John Paul appears breathlessly. 'He's gone now,' he says.

'Are you sure?' says Freddy with a look of relief.

'Does Franky know?'

'Know what?' I say.

'Ah nothin''

'What are you going to do with your day?' I ask.

'Things.'

'Stay out of trouble,' I say.

'Stay out of cars,' says Freddy.

'You don't like cars?'

'No.'

'I don't like cars either.'

'Do you not, Franky?' says Freddy taking interest.

'My mother was killed by a car.'

'Jez.'

'Yeah, when I was your age.'

'Smashed up?' says John Paul.

'Yeah.'

'Jez.'

'But tell me why *you* don't like cars?'

'That's a long story, Franky. Maybe some other time.'

Freddy looks at John Paul.

'It *is* a long story, Franky.'

A long story, that adult-speak again.

'Do you want some batteries, Franky?' Freddy says, removing one of the bulges from a trouser pocket.

'Uncharged?' I say.

They pause, look at one another, laugh. 'That's a good one, Franky.'

A man with a walrus moustache in a tweed cap and overcoat trudges towards the desk.

My dad. Dad takes a free bus ride to the library with his pension pass if he misses me at a weekend. He hands me his notebook. I open a page containing my own printing. HOW ARE YOU DAD? DID YOU LOCK THE FRONT DOOR AFTER YOU? It's the same page I open every time we meet. Dad sometimes forgets to lock the door. He leaves the lock on the latch and forgets to take it off. It's the same non-conversation we have on every occasion. Time doesn't exist between Dad and me.

He examines the note as if it is a hieroglyph and looks at me with pleading eyes. He's just here to see that I'm here, to check on each other's existence as it were.

'THERE ARE NICE LAMB CHOPS IN BUCKLEY'S,' I write. I saw them in their window on my way to work. I worry about Dad, hope he's eating proper meals, although Mrs Dempsey keeps a regular eye on him. He scrutinises the new note. Is he going to say anything or just slouch off as he did last time, like old Mr what'shisname who didn't know the day.

'Lamb chops?' he says.

I nod, smiling, glad to hear him speak.

'I might try one,' he says.

With the rolls of wallpaper under my oxter I call to the Diamond after work. I put the wallpaper down by the counter and order a Bushmills from Jimmy the barman. The pub is almost full. Three girls in bikinis are dancing to the sound of disco music on a tiny stage at the back. I look closely. Yes it is her. The girl in the middle *is* Sandra.

I feel let down. The window exhibition was not special after all. It was just a rehearsal for this vulgar display (she is even using her hands in the same way as she did in her room). But at least I can say George was wrong: they are not strippers; they are dancers. I look around. I want to tell George that to his face. I want him to be absolutely clear about the difference, but there is no sign of him.

I finish my drink and am about to leave when a potbellied male seated near me shouts, 'Hey, Judy in the middle, give us a peep.'

'Her name isn't Judy,' I say.

'Wha'?'

I walk towards the exit. The man, in a delayed reaction, shouts after me, 'How would you fuckin' know anyhow?'

Myrtle very nearly upsets the architectural symmetry of her kitchen when I arrive home without the wallpaper. She grabs a ladle off a stand, and threatening me with it, drives me out the door. 'And don't come back without it,' she shouts. 'I can't rely on you for anything.'

I walk away in silence, leaving her frothing at the mouth. She's become almost comical now, like something out of a cartoon. The silent treatment is best, I have found. Arguing with her when she's like that only makes her worse. Human error (when it's somebody else's) is not in Myrtle's script.

I breathe in the cool air as I walk down the avenue. Back and forth, up and down, that's my yo-yo life. I pass by young girls under lamplight who chant as they skip, drawing the dying drops out of the evening. They are immortalising Myrtle in a ditty.

'Ballcutter, Ballcutter on the rampage

Ballcutter, Ballcutter jump from your cage.'

and one girl jumps out from the rope. I go over to them and, to their consternation, shake one of their hands and say, 'Good on you, girls.'

Back in the pub, the dancers have gone and the drinkers' interest is directed towards the rolls of wallpaper. A roll has been opened and spread on the floor near the potbellied man's stool. He is looking down at the wallpaper discussing its design and texture, shouting comments across the counter to Jimmy.

'Paper roses,' he slobbers, trying to sing.

In my haste to retrieve the paper, my elbow collides with a pint glass of Guinness on the counter which inverts and spews upon the wallpaper.

'It's your man,' says the potbellied male. 'Where are ya goin' to put the roses?' he mocks, swaying on his stool as I struggle with the rolls out the door.

I never saw a woman so drawn and woebegone as Noreen Browne. She stands at her door and gives me a wan smile and I smile back. She looks as if life has sucked her dry and left her as a coat and a hat and a handbag hanging on a bony frame. I can see the skeleton in her face like that of a famine victim. What hunger, what want is starving her?

There were rows. I could hear them through the walls. The shouting was so clear at one stage that I imagined that there were no walls, that it was only paper that separated our houses. And I wondered was that the way it was meant to be, was that the way we were meant to live cheek by jowl with others? Noreen was no match for George. George was always louder than Noreen, just like Myrtle is always louder than me.

Tonight I'm reading in bed. Myrtle is asleep (thankfully this time. I won't repeat the words she used when she saw the condition of the wallpaper but at least they were only words on this occasion). I hear traffic on the road beyond the avenue and then I can just make out Noreen's voice meekly pleading. George has come home late. I heard the gate and now I hear the door being banged. I hear words like 'this hour,' and then George saying, 'Fuck the hour, what difference does the hour make when I come home here?' I hold the book tightly. Myrtle moans, turns but doesn't waken. Something about France is mentioned and then I hear something being smashed and a child's voice (Freddy's) imploring, 'Don't do it, Daddy. Don't do it, Daddy,' over and over. And then I hear a loud bang against the dividing wall.

I stay awake. I sip water from my glass. I'm a light sleeper at the best of times. Noreen is weeping, her sobs, like rain, seeping through walls. I hear a front door slam and a gate creak and I look out my bedroom window and I see George marching down the avenue with an overcoat hanging over his shoulders. He looks like a military officer the way he steps it out and the way the coat hangs like a cloak. I look at my watch. It is four fifteen.

I go into the study. I skim through pages of a couple of books for a while and then I see Sandra in her window. I turn off the light. She is looking behind her and moving away as if someone has summoned her. She comes back to the blind and pulls it down. Someone has come into the room. I can just make out the outline on the blind before the lights are dimmed, the outline of a man.

There's a chill in the air as I return to the bedroom. I put on a dressing gown and sit by the window to keep vigil on the avenue. There is no point in going back to bed and just lying there listening to Myrtle groaning. She groans a lot in her sleep; it's like she's releasing all the toxins she has stored up in the daytime.

I stare out at the misty street lamps, and the trees denuded now, and the increasing pile in the carpet of leaves. I see frost forming on the window pane, water transforming into crystal ice and I think how the world must always change. If the tadpole never became a frog, if the caterpillar always remained in its chrysalis, there would be no continuity in things, everything would stay in a rut like the way it is with Myrtle and me.

I see the stars fading and the dawn come up, breaking through the thick canopy of darkness, slowly pushing with all its might to be born, to declare the day.

And all the time I watch. But George Browne does not return.

There was commotion on the avenue the day Freddy died. Older people walked back and forth wailing. Young people were numbed and silent. A fire brigade came to bring down his body.

'The ball got caught in the pylon and he went climbing up to get it. That's how it happened. That's what Ida said.'

'How does *she* know? Was *she* there?' I'm annoyed that Ida always has information before me, particularly this time. I mean what did she care about Freddy? This time I should have known first.

'I told you something bad would come out of that pylon,' Myrtle says, ignoring my questions, 'but no one would listen.'

I feel remorseful that I hadn't given Freddy his ball when he asked for it. And now I feel remorseful that I'd given the ball back at all. If I hadn't given the ball back, Freddy would not have been found drooped lifeless on a high rung of the pylon.

Then I think that maybe the flap of his boot got caught in some way. He never bought the new boots or got his old ones repaired.

Or the chestnut trees. If they had not been felled, he would have had them to climb instead and maybe... who knows?

I look across at George standing at the grave. He stands straight and tall, with dignity, is what we are expected to say for a man who hides or controls emotion. Of course Myrtle would say there was no emotion there in the first place. But what would she know?

The kids of the avenue, all spruced up in their best-behaviour clothes, form a guard of honour as the child-size coffin is lowered into the earth.

The world sheds many tears. I shed one or two myself for

Freddy, rascal or not there was something about him, a personality trying to appear precociously worldlywise. But it was his cry of pain that night through the wall that made my heart go out to him. We never had a child, Myrtle and I, other than the miscarriage. I would have liked to have baptised that little creature, to have given it a burial in a little box, a ceremony instead of a dumping which is what Ida gave it. Myrtle said the doctor told her that what Ida did was all right. Not having a kid of my own was part of the reason I suppose why Freddy started to grow on me, and especially when I learned he was having a rough time. The kid didn't even know when it was rough; he had nothing to contrast it with. I could have taken more of an interest in him, could have brought him to the mountains or the sea or even the cinema the odd time. Anywhere other than the avenue. I could really have got to like that kid.

Myrtle and Ida stand firm and solemn, arms interlinked, eyeing the proceedings, catching every nuance of emotion and expression in others – the slightest differentiation stored up for the mythology liquidiser later on. And yet, for their part, there is nothing revelatory in either woman, apart from a tightening of Myrtle's arm around Ida's, and Ida's intermittently twitching eye. Or nothing to be read from George's face either. Myrtle keeps staring over at him, trying to fathom him, and he throws the odd look across at her.

We move with the mourners to the Diamond. Pubs are essentially designed for mourners or moaners (who are simply people on a different level of mourning). Moaning was all I ever heard there when as a kid I went to fetch my father home. Elderly men weeping into dark liquids. The modern music scenario there is simply a superficial gloss to cover a pool filled with men's tears. And I wondered if perhaps alcoholics cry easily because of the heightened emotions induced by the drug. But then I think of my father. Of the hopeless silence of a man's tears.

Sometimes names intimate the opposite of what things are. The Diamond is a seedy, run-down place. Seats are torn and there are old cigarette burns on the red plastic upholstery. There are no windows. The place is devoid of any lustre and yet it is called the Diamond. It's like Myrtle insisting on calling our house on the avenue Mountain View, when there is no trace of a mountain. Just the pylon.

Myrtle as per usual is munching crisps and drinking bottled Guinness. Ida, with crucifixes suspended from her ears, is sitting near her in the company of neighbours.

'Such a waste.'

'Such a young boy.'

'I knew it would all lead to something like this.'

Myrtle is looking over at George.

'Didn't I say it would all lead to something?' she says louder. I even said it to Francis. Didn't I, Francis?'

I refuse to answer. I see John Paul and Tomo standing at the door of the pub and I unfurl my handkerchief to get coins to buy them lemonade. The handkerchief is crinkled and frayed. Ida is staring across at me. She is gloating; she is telling me by that look that she knows that Myrtle refuses to wash hankies. She knows Myrtle keeps telling me to use paper ones, but I like the cotton, so I wash them myself but don't bother to iron them. The cotton keeps coins from rattling and keys from making holes. Ida is gloating because she is privy to domestic secrets between Myrtle and me, because she knows that there is nothing I can do about their shared confidences at my expense.

The coins extricated, the handkerchief returned quickly to the pit of my trouser pocket, I pay for the lemonade and go over to the boys. The boys smell as if they have been disinfected. They are probably in their Confirmation clothes. John Paul's hair is gelled. A cowlick sticks out on top of his head. His is the sort of hair which, no matter how much you slap down, no matter how much oil or gel you use, it will keep popping up again defiantly like a recalcitrant weed.

'Thanks, Franky.'

'Thanks, Franky.'

'Are you all right, lads? I'm sorry about Freddy,' I say.

'Will you help us get him, Franky?' says Tomo.

'Get who?' I deliberately refrain from saying *whom*.

'Spikey.'

'Yeah,' says John Paul, 'we want to do him in.'

'A round over here,' Myrtle shouts to me as she heads towards the *Ladies*. 'It's ordered, all you have to do is pay for it.'

All you have to do. It's always *all you have to do*. Myrtle pushes into George. Their lips move *at* each other. They are out of my hearing but by their expressions (grimaces, clenched teeth), it is clear that they are not words of sympathy that pass between them.

I bring Myrtle and Ida their tray of Guinness. I am resentful. Why am I spending money particularly on this Ida one who just mocks me all the time? But I deliver the tray nonetheless, anything to avoid hassle.

'George should see the Council over that pylon,' says Ida as Myrtle returns.

There are crow's feet under Ida's eyes and protuberant veins on the backs of her hands.

'A disgrace, that's what it is,' says Myrtle.

After a few more Guinness they tire of talking about Freddy and the pylon, and Myrtle is telling some neighbours about a fight Ida got into with a man, an elderly drunk who unfortunately for him happened to be stumbling along the avenue.

'He pulled out his *thing* at Ida.'

'He must've been blind drunk,' I say.

'The filthy get, going to the toilet right in front of her.'

'Going to the toilet?' I say.

'No respect for women. Ida let fly at him, didn't you Ida?'

'I sure did.'

'She kicked him and punched him and knocked him flat on his face. She said if she'd had her hand bag with her she'd have taken out her scissors and cut his *thing* off altogether, wouldn't

47

you Ida?'

'I sure would.'

'A woman has to stand up for herself.'

'But he didn't stick it out *at* her,' I say

Myrtle gives me one of her looks. 'You're always trying to twist things,' she says. 'He stuck it out and got what was coming to him.'

Mr what'shisname appears swaying outside the *Gents* with his face bruised.

'That's him,' points out Ida, her crucifixes dancing. 'That's the drunk pervert.'

Since Freddy's funeral, Myrtle has gone into a frenzy of domestic activity. She's changing the house from top to bottom. She has replaced the dining room suite and the lino in the kitchen and she's scraping wallpaper off every wall. And then she suddenly stops in the middle of it all and announces that she is going on a holiday.

'Ida says I need a break after all that happened.'

'*Ida says*. What's it to you what happened? You never liked the kid.'

'Don't get me started,' she says.

'And what about the mess?' I say, looking at the state of the house.

'You can do that,' she says

'And when are you going?' I say.

'Tonight,' she says. 'Ida just got the tickets.'

'Tonight?'

'Yeah. It's only for a week.'

'And where is it you might be going to?'

'An island in Greece.'

'And what might the name of the island be?'

'The name escapes me now,' she says, putting her hand on her temple in a half-hearted effort at remembrance. 'Ida says there's great travel bargains at this time of year.'

'She does, does she?'

'Yeah.'

'And who's paying for all of this?'

'Ida's paying.'

And that's all she says, because the next thing I know she is going out the door pulling her already packed suitcase behind her on its little wheels.

A quiet has descended on the avenue. The kids, except for the really small ones, go around like ghosts, silent, no chanting, no play, as if a pall is covering everything. Solemn, stealth-like going in and out of doors. Bouquets of flowers placed near the pylon – ironic, as if the pylon is the one being venerated. A cold wind blows up the avenue. I shudder. Alone. A wife where? Doing what? Do I really care? An empty house. Bare walls. Peace.

After a few days there is the sound of play again. A ball lands in my garden. I puncture it with a kitchen knife, tear it apart, ravage it until all that's left are little strips of plastic worth a human life. I get a bad name with the kids. John Paul and Tomo look at me as if I've grown horns. They chant with the other kids, 'Ballcutters, ballcutters' (in the plural now) outside forty eight. Fickleness. There are some new kids who don't know about Freddy or the pylon, but John Paul and Tomo were Freddy's mates and they have no memories. I don't care about the name-calling. It's for their own good I'm doing it. They don't understand.

And then one evening another ball lands in the front garden. I don't know where it came from. The kids are playing down the far end of the avenue. No one comes to claim it. When I split the ball open I find a bag of smack inside. I don't get excited. I just coolly walk down to the prefabricated building which is the garda station and hand it in, and the ruddy-complexioned sergeant, equally cool, takes down the details and says it is a grand mild evening and then the phone rings, and not to worry a bit, he says, picking up the phone, that the matter is already under investigation.

I answer the front door. It's Saturday, early evening. Mrs Dempsey is standing there in an open overcoat holding a cake. 'I thought you might like it, Francis. The apples are fresh from the garden. I was next door looking in on Noreen, doing a couple of things for her. She's not right at all, that misfortunate woman. Wasn't it terrible about poor Freddy?'

She waddles into the kitchen looking around at Myrtle's art exhibits hanging, looking for spots, dust particles perhaps that she could wipe up. 'It's not fair,' she's saying, putting the tart on the table, 'the way some people suffer'.

'Will you have cup of tea, Mrs Dempsey?'

'I won't, Francis. I had a cuppa in Noreen's. I just wanted to look in and see how you were getting on.'

'I'm fine.'

She looks at me, waiting, hoping perhaps that I will fill her in with some details

'It's terrible,' she says, 'what some people get away with.'

I'm not sure if she's referring to George or Myrtle.

She sighs. 'You *are* looking after yourself?'

'I am.'

'Will you come around for dinner one of these days?'

'I'd like that, Mrs Dempsey.'

'Soon?'

'Soon.'

She smiles, happy with that. 'I better be on my way.'

'I'll walk you home.'

'Ah, you don't have to be doing that, Francis.'

'It's no problem. I want to look in on Dad anyway.'

'God be good to him, the poor man.'

We walk along the avenue or rather I walk and Mrs Dempsey

51

waddles stiffly, linking me.

'You don't mind me holding onto you, Francis.'

'Not at all,' I say. I find it comforting in fact. Companionable.

'I do be afraid sometimes, Francis. There are dreadful things happening. Those cider-drinkers and drug addicts; all the drugs, I don't know what the world's coming to.'

I hold back from telling Mrs Dempsey about what I had found in the football.

When we reach the cottages I see the light on in my father's bedroom.

'He'll be asleep,' she says. 'What time is it? He goes to bed early, at the first sign of darkness. He does forget to turn off the light.'

'I wont waken him so,' I say, releasing her grip at her garden gate. 'I'll just check his front door is locked.'

Darkness has fallen as I make my way home. The days are growing increasingly shorter, the evenings quickening in. A new if temporary freedom unfolds in front of me. But it's still only an empty house that beckons. I'm hungry. I'm musing to myself whether to cook for supper or whether to make do with Mrs Dempsey's apple tart, when I see a girl walking towards me. My heart skips a beat for under the streetlight I recognise her as Sandra. She is eating chips from white greaseproof paper. As she draws close I see her eyes are moist. I'm annoyed she doesn't look at me. She doesn't recognise me from Adam. I want to get through to her in some way. I could open up a conversation by asking why there are tears in her eyes. Instead I flash a smile and say, 'Any chance of a chip?' I don't know why I say that. It's cheap, non-classy, not even adult-speak. But as soon as I say the words, fists shoot out from the darkness and knock me to the ground. Fists with knuckles metal-spiked to penetrate my chin.

I'm not rendered quite unconscious. I hear a voice saying, 'What are you fuckin' wastin' time with him for? There's people waitin' for you.'

I feel fingers tingling against my chest. I'm too weak to move.

A hand going through my inside pocket removes my wallet. I hear another blow and a girl's voice shouts in an English accent. 'That's it Spikey. That's the fuckin' last straw.'

The gardaí find me lying on the side of the road, a few hundred yards from the avenue. So near to home. They're different gardaí to the ones I saw in the station. Two young guys, early twenties, mannerly. 'You could've been hit by a vehicle, sir, the way you were left.' I want them to search the streets right away. 'First things first, sir.'

They bring me to casualty in Blanchardstown hospital where I had the knee job done. I get a couple of stitches in my chin. 'That was opened with something sharper than a fist, man,' the black student doctor says.

I nearly throw up.

'Are you all right?'

'It's the hospital smells, the smell of ether or something. I get nauseated.'

'You'll be all right, man,' he says, 'we don't use ether now.'

The young gardaí are waiting for me in the waiting room. 'Is it very painful, sir?' We search the streets in the squad-car. I'm only half alert. I kept repeating to myself: assaulted over a chip, a salted chip. I run the words together. I keep saying the words, assaulted chip like a mantra, keep naming the thing so I can have a handle to hold on to.

We cut back towards the avenue. There is no one to be found in the ghostly streets, except for the odd couple of ravelled lovers returning from a disco or a solitary drunk stumbling along.

There are whispers on the avenue about the Ballcutter's husband knowing Judy. When I walk out to work or come home in the evening there is a wink and a nudge as I pass by.

John Paul and Tomo and some of the other kids ignore me now. Apart from cutting up their footballs, they also think I'm in league with the cider-drinkers because I had something to do with Judy.

I sit on the garden wall in the evenings even though it is colder now. I offer sweets to the kids of the avenue, but they snub me. They walk past me muttering things like 'scab' or 'Judy's ride' and some of them still chant, 'Ballcutter' under their breath. 'Ballcutter.' That epithet seems so mild now.

I keep going out to the wall. I keep offering sweets to the kids. I ignore the taunts. Eventually they die down when there is no response. I become the garden gnome with sweets hanging out of my pocket, and after a time the younger kids come forward, the innocent kids who have only hazy, garbled versions of the incident, who are at a stage where a taste for sweets is stronger than any ideological loyalty. These kids come forward slowly, unlocking their palms.

John Paul and Tomo pass near, disapproving yet curious at the same time.

'Do you want to hear the story?' I say.

'You're just a fucker,' says John Paul.

'Look at my chin.' I show them the scar. 'I had to be stitched.'

'How many stitches?' says Tomo.

'Twenty,' I say exaggerating. 'Do you think a friend would do this?'

'It was Spikey,' says John Paul.

'Melancholy bit his hand,' says Tomo.

'He had a steel hand,' I say.

'Steel?'

'Yeah.'

'Jez.'

They draw a little closer to examine my chin, gradually losing their distrust.

'I was coming home from the Diamond. This girl was passing by. I didn't know her, I swear. I said nothing, not a word to her, and then he jumped me, the cider-drinker. I didn't know her at all.'

'It was Spikey.'

'It had to be him.'

'You know by the scar.'

'Look, I'm really sorry about Freddy. I really liked him. If I hadn't given him the ball, he might be...'

'That's why you cut the footballs up now, isn't it Franky?' says John Paul. 'It's for Freddy, isn't it?'

'Yes,' I say.

'It wasn't *you*,' Tomo says. 'It was Spikey. He got even with Melancholy. He had to get even with Freddy as well.'

'What do you mean?'

'He threw the ball.'

'Into the pylon,' says John Paul.

'He sees Freddy playin' that evenin'. He comes up and takes his ball and starts examin' it and then, as if disappointed with something, says, "Fuck" and throws it into the pylon. The ball stays up over the wire mesh, near the barbed wire. It doesn't burst. Freddy climbs up as far as the wire, but he can't reach the ball, so he climbs up higher. He goes above the wire and he reaches out to get the ball and then he looks down and sees Spikey taking out his knife and grinning up at him; and Spikey starts paring his nails with the knife. And instead of coming down, Freddy climbs up higher, holding the ball in one hand.'

'And the ball slips out of his hand,' says John Paul.

'And Freddy looks down to see if Spikey is still there, and Spikey is still there with the knife grinnin' up, and Freddy climbs up further and he goes up very high.'

'And then his foot slips...'

'And he falls, and his body lands on a rung and he slumps over like there were two halves of him on either side of the rung. He shouts out, but what can we do? It all happens so quick. His legs and hands are danglin' and his head is rockin', and then all of a sudden all the parts of him stop movin', and he just hangs there.'

'And Spikey walks off.'

'And all the warning signs,' I say, 'the yellow arrows and the big letters saying, DANGER. HIGH VOLTAGE. Nobody could miss them.'

'Who reads those things?'

'No fuckin' good,' says John Paul.

'Do his parents know all this?' I say.

'His oul fella doesn't give a fuck.'

'What's the point in tellin' *them?*'

'No point now.'

M yrtle and Ida are home from their holiday. I wouldn't have cared about their coming back at all were it not for the incident. They haven't seen me yet since they returned. I come home after working late on new requisitions for the library and there's this note on the kitchen table saying they have gone to bingo. That's typical. They write an epistle to say they're going a few hundred yards down the road but sweet nothing when it comes to flying off thousands of miles in an aeroplane.

The incident is the bother. I expect a drama when Myrtle returns. She won't see the scar or sense the pain. Oh no. Myrtle will just heed the Chinese whispers.

I look at Myrtle's and Ida's snapshots which were left on the table. I see Myrtle and Ida drinking wine. Myrtle and Ida on the beach. Myrtle and Ida in a boat. Myrtle in a mauve bikini putting suncream on her wobbly bits. Myrtle lying on her tummy with a tiny white rectangle protruding from her bikini bottom at the small of her back. Myrtle and Ida suntanned, smiling into candlelight.

'We heard,' she says accusingly, coming in the door, pulling her wheelie case behind her. Ida, grinning from ear to ear, is in her wake holding a cheroot with a long ash. She pops into the sitting room leaving the door open. She will listen with ears cocked for a kitchen drama to unfold. Myrtle is wearing a white blouse, the short sleeves showing off her tan and huge brown freckles.

'What did you hear?' I say.

'Trying to take advantage,' she says, leaving her case down and surveying her kitchen, her little empire, looking for flaws there as well.

'What are you talking about?' I'm standing in the kitchen

doorway leaning against the architrave.

'A young girl like that.'

'What?'

'You were seen in the Diamond.'

'Who saw me?'

'Lots of people.'

'I was just drinking.'

'Ida says you asked Judy out for a meal.'

'*Ida says*,' I mimic. 'How would she know what I asked?'

'You don't even know.'

'Know what?'

'Judy is Ida's niece, you gobshite.'

A loud laugh from Ida through the open door.

Myrtle goes into the sitting-room. I follow. I want her to explain, to elaborate on the connection between Ida and Judy, but Ida is sitting there on my armchair gloating, pretending to preen herself, admiring her tan.

'I go away for a week and I come back to this.'

'A holiday,' I say. 'You went away on a holiday. Ida do you mind?'

She won't move from the armchair. She won't get out of my house. It's since the holiday this is happening. This is a more developed type of effrontery now. Normally she takes the hint and buzzes off.

'Tell her to get out,' I say to Myrtle.

'I won't tell her to get out. Why should I tell her to get out?'

Ida beams up at me.

I feel my anger rising. 'I'll make her get out,' I say approaching her, my fists gnarled tightly at my sides.

Ida, still grinning, takes a scissors from her handbag.

'Make me, Frank,' she says showing me the point.

A drop of sweat trickles down my cheek. They're waiting. I stand hovering for a moment, staring at a usurper's boxer's nose. Myrtle is poised behind me, silent for once, but I can feel her breathing loud and quick. I say nothing more. I turn on my heel, brush past Myrtle and walk out of the room. The two of them burst out laughing as I go out, a sneering laugh of victory. Myrtle shouts after me, 'Go and get your oul fella.'

I go to the Diamond and start drinking pints of Guinness. One after another. I down a pint in three gulps. The potbellied male arrives. 'Your usual, Enda?' Jimmy shouts to him. The dancers are starting their act. Sandra/Judy is bopping in her pink bikini, strutting her stuff.

Enda half-looks at me. 'How's it goin' with *Judy*?' (He emphasises the name). 'Did you give her the roses?'

The alcohol is swimming around in my brain. I'm feeling lightheaded. *The Unbearable Lightness of Being.* A good title that by Kundera. I think of the Americans. *a shot, a hit, hit me with a shot.*

'Hit me with a shot,' I shout at Jimmy. 'Makes sure it's Bushmills.'

Jimmy is sharp. He spent some time in the States. Knows all the terms. Didn't always though. I remember years ago Myrtle asked for a *Screwdriver* (she didn't really want the drink; it was just to show off), and he thought something needed fixing. He was right in a way. Something did need fixing, only I didn't know. Jimmy is a small bloke but tough and muscular. Does weights in the gym in the Centre. Takes no shit from anyone except from Spikey, or so the story goes. His sleeky hair is parted in the middle and he wears a wine-coloured waistcoat which makes him look like a professional gambler or casino owner from a Wild West movie. His sleeves are always rolled up, ready for work or trouble.

'A double shot,' I say.

Jimmy smiles and tops up my glass.

I feel the warmth of the whiskey entering my stomach. I feel strong. I could have flattened her, Ida I mean. She's not a woman. And these louts. I could flatten them.

'Oooh,' says Enda, as the girls turn and bend to the beat of a noisy rock tune. 'Get them off you.'

'The length of the pins,' someone shouts.

The girls give a high kick.

'They go all the way up.'

'Fuck sake'

'Do you know who I am?' I say, my temper rising.

Enda takes a long swig from his Guinness.

'Do we know who you are?' He shouts to the smiling Jimmy. 'Do we know who he is? We know all about you. You're Franky Copeland from the avenue. You live near George. Do you know George? Always chasing the skirt is George.'

He barks out a laugh. 'Must be something in the air where you guys live.'

'What are you talking about?' I say irately.

'You were trying to have it off with Judy, remember?'

Things are no longer staying still. Enda is swaying in front of me. 'You're a liar,' I say.

'Spikey's over there,' he says threateningly. 'Maybe I should call him over.'

I feel the empty glass in my hand.

'Spikey,' shouts Enda.

I smash the glass on Enda's bald head and pull the stool from under him. 'Scandal monger.'

The music stops. The dancers stand motionless, covering themselves with their arms, as I push my way out past formerly loud and wolf-whistling men in big coats and caps, now reduced to silence.

I walk down one street and then another and another aimlessly. I avoid the avenue. I make sure, no matter how drunk I am, that I avoid the avenue. At all costs. Then I say I shouldn't avoid the avenue. I should go back to my home and claim my rights.

Instead I wander. I go down by the canal. It's quiet. Some of the light from the street lamps sends a sheen over the water near the bridge. I see the cider-drinkers on the other side of the canal at a distance. Seven or eight of them at least. They are gathered around a fire. I hear them laughing. They see me. They throw stones – too far away to find their target. They taunt me. I don't know exactly what they are saying, but I know they are taunts. I can see it in their gestures, their fingers in the air, the wide hollow of their mouths.

I walk on. It's quite dark now. No moon or stars are shining. I keep walking. I don't know how far I walk or for how long. I feel fatigued. I don't think I can walk anymore. My legs, they just refuse to take any more orders. I slump down with my back against a low wall. My lids are closing. My little blinds. To blot out a world.

I open my eyes to see big Doc Martens stationary in front of me. George is shaking my arm. He says he was out for a walk to clear his head or something like that. I tell him I can't go home. He doesn't ask any questions. He makes no comment on the state of my chin which is smarting as he helps me to my feet.

All he says is, 'You must've had some mixture.'

I can't remember passing through the avenue. Maybe it's just as well. What must I have looked like? What must the kids have thought if they saw me at that time? George puts me to bed in a small boxroom; it's Freddy's room; there's a photograph beside the bed of Freddy with his arms around his dog. 'George,' I say. 'Tell me about Freddy.' 'You go to bed now,' he says. 'Sleep it off.'

I'm on the other side of the wall of my own house. A strange feeling that, like you've been turned inside out or back to front. This is where all the cryptic sounds had come from. It's silent in here now with Freddy gone and Noreen back in hospital (she took a turn for the worse, not surprising after Freddy' death). It's like I'm lying in his cemetery, profaning it, not knowing what really went on, left to wonder.

I am one massive headache. It happened once before, pain of such intensity I mean. It wasn't due to drink. It was after sex with Myrtle – such a rare thing perhaps befuddling the brain, making it cry out from shock, causing a rumble through redundant capillaries. I turn sideways on the pillow and face the dividing wall of two houses, of two sets of lives or maybe more. I hear a scraping sound coming from the other side of the wall. It's Myrtle taking off the old wallpaper. *Scrape, scrape.* The sound pierces my nerves, adding to the hangover.

I hear Ida's husky laugh. They're cracking some joke. Probably laughing at me. Ida with her scissors trying to snip the thread of man's destiny, and I think of the slit between her legs and wonder if she considers it as something inflicted.

Do they know I'm on the other side of these eight-by-fours, only feet away? Did they see me coming in? It wouldn't have bothered them. They wouldn't have cared if I'd spent the night on skid row.

There is music playing now. Greek music. The balalaika. Now it's Myrtle's turn to laugh, more high-pitched, more screechy like the laugh of someone being tickled.

The scraping has stopped. The laughing has stopped. All I can hear now is the sound of the balalaika.

George has left me his house key and a note. He has to go down the country to install some machines. He says when he gets back he'll talk to me about the cider-drinkers. That's the nearest he got to acknowledging his son's murder.

I make my way unsteadily to George's bathroom and find some paracetemol in his cabinet which I wash down with a tumbler of bathroom water. I shave with George's razor, skimming around the stitched part of my chin.

Why did Myrtle marry me? That's all I keep asking myself as I walk out George's gate. I feel so strange walking parallel to my own garden, parallel to my former life. It's like I've come out of my own skin, a sort of clone, and maybe I'll see the other me any minute now coming out the door of my own house.

I look up at my bedroom window but the curtains are drawn. They have blotted me out of their world as if they are a powerful government airbrushing me out of history. I'm passing the bus stop. Why did she marry at all? I say it partly audibly, sibilantly like Mrs Dempsey's praying in the church. An elderly woman on the queue looks at me – the woman with the brolly. She smiles understandingly.

'You have to offer it all up, love.'

Offer it all up. Grin and bear it. That was the old way. Who would do that now?

I walk on, my head feeling light. Why did I marry her? What did I see in her, or she in me? 'A gobshite,' that's what Ida called me on my wedding day. I told Myrtle. But all she said was, 'Don't mind her.' 'But it's our wedding day,' I said, 'and she's saying stuff like this.' 'She doesn't mean any harm.' Any harm? What's harm if that's not harm?

And now Myrtle herself is calling me these names.

All the years with my head buried in books, like an ostrich, that's what Myrtle said, and it suited her down to the ground. The world was covered. It never sloughed off its caul for me. There were chinks I suppose, intimations – more than that – which I never followed up. A bit lazy perhaps (a bit like my father?). Resigned to see no evil, hear no evil. My life would probably have just continued in its wont were it not for the incident. And Ida's constant encroaching of course. And the holiday. Let's not forget the holiday.

I was her front. I see it now. I hadn't a clue. My marriage to her made her look respectable on the avenue, and all the time she could be 'doing the other', whatever the other was. Rock Hudson. I remember she talked about him when he died, how his marriage was contrived to cover up his secret propensities, his 'musical preferences'. 'That's *men* for you,' she said.

We went to the cinema a lot in the early days – the little local cinema down the Centre which is no more. Hudson affected me too. Saw all his films. Looked up to him as this hero, this all American male. He botched up my notions of machismo and chivalry and all that sort of stuff. Hard to believe that one man could do that. But he did (with consolation at a later stage of course from Myrtle and Ida). See it depends when it hits you. He hit me at an impressionable age. The Rock of Gibraltar, that's what he was named after, as solid as that, and it didn't dawn on me for one moment that a rock might have fissures or that a river might not run true. And I remember his leading ladies like the beautiful Jennifer Jones, caring, gentle, feminine, whom I beheld from a darkened room as the ideal of womanhood, the missing rib, the provider of man's (Rock's) completion. And I thought that was the way it was. The model to go by, with Myrtle wrapped around me in the back seat teaching me French kissing, keeping me on constant simmer.

A television crew with a van and lights and cameras is setting up near the pylon. The avenue has become an item of news since Freddy's death; it has entered a larger world.

From the window of Freddy's room I see a candlelight vigil taking place around the pylon. People are walking in a circle, some of them carrying placards which I can't read because of the dark. They are chanting something which I can't make out.

There's a painting of a weeping boy on Freddy's wall or rather a copy of a painting, quite large, incongruous in a small boy's room beside the cut-out posters of soccer stars. And of course by the bed, the photograph ..

A small TV set is on a raised shelf in the corner of the room. (Did it come with the batteries?). I switch it on. The sound is toned down. Some man is being interviewed. He speaks as if his mouth is under water and his words are bubbles hitting the surface. Then I see a news reporter lowering a microphone to the lips of John Paul. I turn the volume up. Tomo is standing beside him. John Paul is talking about Freddy. 'What height did he fall from?' the reporter asks. John Paul points. The camera switches to the pylon, panning it slowly, caressing its steel, making it appear innocuous, artistic, almost like the Eiffel Tower. The camera switches back to the children who look like dwarfs in contrast to the previous image. 'And what is your name?' the reporter asks the little plump girl who is now holding her doll in her arms. 'Sue Ellen Mulholland,' the girl replies. Sue Ellen is at last making her TV debut. 'You saw the fall?'

'No,' she says, 'Me mammy called me in.'

Myrtle and Ida are now standing in front of the microphone staring straight out. 'That pylon...' Myrtle is saying in her angry

66

voice. I turn the sound off. I watch them gesticulate like actresses from the silent screen. I watch their expressions of outrage being mocked by the silence. For the first time in my life I'm able to turn Myrtle off. The empowerment of a switch. Myrtle and Ida are now my puppets. Myrtle is gesticulating furiously. Ida is nodding, supporting what she is saying. I press the TV switch and obliterate them both.

George has a new car. I presume it's his own and not a company car, because he still drives the van for the condom machines. I haven't seen him much since the funeral. 'I've been away a lot.' That's all he says. No elaboration. Well maybe if I were installing condom machines in pubs around the country I wouldn't elaborate either.

It's Saturday, late morning, and I'm sitting in the front passenger seat. George has invited me for a spin. My seat belt securely fastened. A little apprehensive when I think of his crash and Noreen. He never elaborated on that either. I smell the new plastic and my fears dissipate. I feel secure, panoplied by glass and metal as rain starts to fall and trickle down the windscreen, and wipers sway back and forth hypnotically.

George's radio, which is playing music low, starts to cackle as we pass the pylon and I steal a look at George's nicotine-stained fingers tapping the dash as he steers with one hand and I say, 'There's the pylon.' Maybe it's not the right thing to say like 'Fancy a chip?' but at least it's not an interrogation.

George switches the radio off and shrugs his shoulders. 'There's fuck all can be done about that. How is Myrtle taking it?'

I'm surprised by the question. I mean why should Myrtle be taking it any differently or any more or any less than anyone else? I mean she couldn't stand the kid, and yet she was angry, not so much about Freddy's death, it seemed to me, but about the pylon. She directed all her anger into the pylon as if the pylon were the scapegoat for everything; the way Freddy was neglected, his truancies, his pilfering were all due to the pylon.

'She's campaigning to get rid of the pylon,' I say.

George laughs cynically. 'That's Myrtle all right. She always wants to get rid of things after the damage is done.'

We drive out of the avenue and down towards the canal. A used condom, like a weather bane, is stuck in a briar. George slows to watch a stray horse with a dirty white mane chomp the sparse grass, wading through and sometimes kicking with his hoof the beer cans and burnt-out fires and used syringes and brown plastic cider flagons, dented or punctured.

'You have to get on with things,' George says.

I don't feel warm anymore in the car. There is cold air blowing somewhere.

'Is there a window open, George?'

'It's the air conditioning. Good, what?'

'There *is* something that can be done about it, George.'

'I'll turn it off if you like.'

'I don't mean the air conditioning.'

'What are you talking about?'

'I'm talking about Freddy's death.'

'What's done is done. You can't bring the dead back.'

'It wasn't an accident. It was murder.'

'What?'

'A cider-drinker murdered Freddy. *Your* son, George.'

A car's horn blares at George as he pulls over to the side of the road. 'Fuck off,' he shouts and glares at the passing motorist. He yanks the handbrake up fiercely, almost pulling it out of the floor. There is no danger of rolling. We are on a level.

Suddenly there are tears in his eyes.

'Are you all right, George?'

'*Am I all right*? You come along and tell me Freddy was murdered and you ask me if I'm all right. *Murdered*. In the name of God.'

'The kids told me. A cider-drinker caused Freddy to fall. A guy called Spikey.'

George sighs.

'Do you know him?' I say.

He pauses.

'George?'

He puts his face down into his hands. 'Do I know him? Jesus Christ he's asking me if I know him.'

I don't press. I sit silently. After a while he lifts his head, sniffles, stares out the windscreen. 'Anyway, that's only hearsay,' he says.

'But all the kids ...'

'Did he lay a finger on him?'

'No, but ...'

'Well then, how could he have killed him if he didn't lay a finger on him? Answer that.'

'There are other ways.'

'What ways?'

'Psychological.'

'Bullshit. The kid fell, end of story.'

'But George ...'

'Just fuck off, okay?'

He takes a swig from a hipflask which he keeps inside his navy blazer. He starts the car again, and soon we're passing bare hedgerows on quieter roads. I'm afraid to press him. Afraid of an outburst. After a few minutes he says, 'I did the best I could for him.'

He takes a bend sharply without slowing down. 'Good torque what?'

'Smooth, George,' I say nervously.

George ponders for a moment. 'You know what I'm going to tell you, Franky? No one knows anyone. We think we do but we're only codding ourselves. No one ever really knows anyone at all.'

The sun comes out catching me uncomfortably in the eyes. I become restless.

'Where are we heading George?'

'Portrane, okay? A bit of sea air?'

'Okay, George.'

He drives fast as we hit the main road. I see a sign saying, SPEED KILLS.

'See the sign, George?'

George laughs and says, 'Are you in the world at all, Franky? Speed means drugs.'

'What?'

'It means drugs fuckin' kill you.'

George takes another swig from his brandy flask. 'Your one takes speed.'

'Who, George?'

'Ah this one. You'd see her if you go down to the Diamond.' He smiles. 'She's fucking expensive though, I'll tell you that, Franky.'

'Expensive?'

He winks. 'She'd cost you an arm and a leg.'

George breaks an amber light coming through Swords. I want to tell him to slow down. But he might take umbrage. I just say, 'We've plenty of time, George.'

He looks at me. He *has* taken umbrage. 'Don't you fucking start sounding like Noreen.'

George is speaking calmly again. 'Do you ever notice, Franky, how things look different from a moving car?' A car that's moving fast I mean. You see women's legs flashing by, a bit of skirt, a bit of stocking, you just see part of them, enough to turn you on, you know what I mean? That's what the street walkers show, just enough to turn a fella on, and houses, all the houses moving, the same oul dead houses that we see every day standing still, and now there they are flashing past; it's exhilarating, Franky; it's like we can leave everything behind us, you know what I'm saying?'

'I know, George.'

George slows down as we come into Portrane. I'm starting to relax when he says, 'I can do a doughnut.'

'What's a doughnut?'

Suddenly he revs hard and spins the car around on its front axle, ignoring the blaring horns of other motorists.

'Fuck sake, George.'

He brings the car to a halt, puts his hands on his thighs and with a self-satisfied look says, 'That's a doughnut.'

We park the car by the low sea wall and walk along the beach. There are no calming waves. The tide is out. But at least that affords us miles of sand to traverse, a desert except for the little pools of water which the sea forgot to take back with it on its return journey. The little pools constitute an obstacle course which we have to surmount. We jump or circumnavigate as the need arises. And I think how long it has been since I got a break away from the avenue or the library, from the holes we dig for ourselves.

'Breathe that air, George.'

I look at George. I smile as I see him alternating between sea air and smoke inhalations from the butt of his cigarette.

A seagull makes its shrill cry over our heads as George lights another cigarette. The flame burns unevenly. He wets the tip of his finger and applies it to the faster burning side of the cigarette, just as Freddy had done. George is a good advertisement for cigarette companies. He hasn't got the slightest wheeze or hoarseness in his voice, not like Ida's gravel.

'It's hard, Franky,' he says exhaling, 'being married to an invalid.'

'She wasn't always an invalid.'

George pauses, looks at me as if to say how would you know.

'There was always something wrong with her. Ah, I should've divorced her but...' He hesitates.

'But what, George?'

'She helped me once. Ah fuck, divorce wasn't on in those days. But any opportunity that presented itself ...' George gives another wink ... 'any bit of fluff that blew my way, you know what I mean?'

'I know, George,' I say, thinking about the stupidity of speculative questions, of trying to anticipate things, of thinking about used johnnies in breast pockets. My mind begins to imagine *bits of fluff*, local tarts.

'You have to be careful of the scissors, George,' I say.

'What?'

'Women who cut men's balls off.'

George laughs. 'You know something, Franky,' he says putting his arm around my shoulders, 'you're all right. What's she like in bed anyway?'

'Who?'

'Myrtle. Sorry I shouldn't be prying.'

'It's all right, George. The truth is things aren't too good in that area.'

'Myrtle wasn't always ... eh so round.'

'You knew her?'

'Of course I knew her. Didn't we all grow up together. She was always great with that Ida one.'

'Great is not the word.'

'I'm going to tell you something, Franky, about that Ida one.'

George looks me in the eye.

'Go ahead, George.'

'Are you ready for it?'

'Shoot.'

'She pisses standing up.'

'What? Ida Hourigan? How do you know?'

George doesn't answer. He just taps the side of his right index finger against his lips.

We walk on in silence for a while, then George says, 'You didn't come out much, did you Franky?'

'How do you mean, George?'

'When you were a lad?'

'Not with the father the way he was.'

'You were a good lad,' he says, taking a swig from his flask, 'looking after your father like that.'

'I often went to the cinema in the Centre.'

'That's the Bingo hall now.'

'I know.'

George caresses his beard. 'Things happen, Franky.' There's a slight slur in his words. 'There's nothing can be done about things that just happen.'

Fine sand races past our feet, fleeing from a gust that has

blown in from the sea. I want to take off my shoes and socks and feel that sand running through my toes, but George would laugh at me, consider me childish. I look down at his Doc Martens leaving heavy imprints in the sand.

'You know maybe you were just as well off,' he says thoughtfully.

'How do you mean, George?'

'Not knowing the half of what went on.'

He lights yet another cigarette and stares out at the horizon. He sings

'Those were the days my friend,
we thought they'd never end,
we'd sing and dance forever and a day.'

and he smiles and says, 'After a swim in the canal we'd take the birds up to the blackberry field. By Jaysus we had fun then.'

'What birds, George?'

'Lots of birds. Rides.'

I want to ask George if Myrtle was among them, but I can't. I can't bring myself to speak now. My chest feels a pressure on it. I'm afraid of what George might answer.

Two blond girls wearing haversacks pass us by, stopping intermittently to pick up shells.

George ogles the girls who are nicely proportioned in blue jeans.

'She's Venus in blue jeans,' George sings.

The girls giggle.

'A bit of all right, what?'

'They look like Swedes,' I say.

He lights another cigarette as the girls circle round with their heads down like birds foraging for morsels.

'I'll take one of those, George.'

'And I'll take the other.'

'No, I mean a cigarette.'

'Oh, I didn't know you ...'

'Maybe I won't. I'll have a mint instead.'

'Jaysus, make up your mind.'

'Would you like one?' I say.

'Are you fucking mad?'

George cups the flame in his two hands but the sea wind blows through his fingers and the flame falters. I wonder will it last long enough to light the cigarette. It brushes against George's finger and thumb, but he shows no sign of pain and holds the match firm, just a piece of charcoal now, as the smoke curls from his cigarette.

'Sweden?' George shouts.

The girls look up

'You from Sweden?'

'Sweden, no. Finland.'

'Ah. Would you like?'

George proffers a cigarette.

'Not me. Only Helvi.'

Helvi is the thinner of the two, the less buxom.

George lights the cigarette from his lighted one and hands it to Helvi.

'Thanks.'

He picks up a large white shell and holds it to his ear.

'The sea, hear,' he says, handing it to Helvi.

Helvi listens to the shell as if she is on a phone, and giggles, and then hands it to the other girl who takes the call and giggles also. The whole thing is absurd. They hold a shell to hear the sea which they can hear without any shell because they are at the sea. And besides, the idea of hearing the sea from a shell is a myth, a distortion of air. Michael in the library told me that.

'Good, yah.' George has changed his accent. He sounds like a German, thinking he sounds like a Finn. He speaks in broken English. I've seen it before. I've seen men talk to foreigners like that, even in the library when they come in looking for information. I am not above blame. Why do we do it? Why do we try to sound like them when they are trying to sound like us?

We walk along beside them. Both girls have perfect skin, pale without a blemish like a Finnish winter.

'Your friend's name?'

'Aino.'

Aino's face is fat, but delectable, like the pudgy fat on a baby, the sort of fat you'd like to eat. She picks up a white stone.

'Many stones you save?' says George.

'Yes.'

'To bring home?'

'Yes.'

To weigh down the aeroplane. To throw away before boarding. To give one something to do so as not to appear conspicuous while walking along a beach, to act as a cover for ulterior motives. Myrtle would have a field day here.

'This is Séamus,' says George, pointing to me.

'Shame us.'

'Yes.'

The girls flash a smile.

'On holiday?' says George.

'Au pair.'

'To learn the English.'

'Helsinki?'

'Yes.'

'Near there.'

'Near there?'

'Outside the city in the suburbia.'

'That's where we live too.'

'In Helsinki?'

'In suburbs. Well, while I'm in Ireland I mean.'

'You Irish?'

'My friend Séamus is.' George rests an arm on my shoulder, 'but I am from America.'

'America?'

'Hollywood.'

'Hollywood?'

'I make films.'

'Ah.'

'Have you ever ..?'

'In film, no.'

'Yes, well once,' says Aino, 'for a ...'

'*Periodique*,' says Helvi.

'You would look good in film,' says George.

The girls giggle.

'I am making film soon.'

The girls giggle again.

'My friend Séamus here is my assistant, my agent in Ireland.'

'Yes?'

'Yes.'

We walk along, out of earshot of traffic now, the noisy world has receded. And we are in a great desert with nobody else about.

Helvi embraces herself. She is cold from the sea breeze.

'They are called dunes,' says George, pointing to the sand hills.

'Dunes,' say the girls and they giggle as if George had hit upon a word in their language, a secret word with connotations.

'Not so cold up there,' says George. 'No breeze.'

We help the girls up the hill of fine shifting sand. They have taken off their runners and tied them with the laces around their necks, and each runner hangs, bumping into each breast as they ascend. I have taken off my shoes too. The girls have given me courage. I can feel the fine granules of sand tickling the inside of my toes, and I think there is something sensual and profoundly free about sand.

George stops in a sheltered dune. He beckons me to go on with Aino while he sits down in the dune with Helvi.

'No wind,' he says.

'You married?' says Helvi.

'My wife is dead,' says George. 'She died in a plane crash two years ago on the eve of Christmas. You know Christmas?'

'Oh yes. I am sorrowful.'

Aino and I move to the next dune. The sand and couch grass

are dry, and we sit on my jacket, but I don't feel warm or comfortable.

'Do you need a johnny?' George shouts and, before I can answer, a packet of condoms lands at my feet.

'Aino laughs.

'Naughty boy,' she says, and throws her arms around me, her blubbery cheeks nearly smothering me.

I hear George grunting and breathing heavily and Helvi still laughing. Is everything in Finland funny?

Aino takes a bottle and a blue beaker from her haversack. She half fills the beaker. Talking about coming prepared. She knocks the drink back in one go. She pours again.

'Now you,' she says.

I gulp the drink down, feeling the warmth in my stomach like Bushmills, but coarser, perhaps more like poitín. I hand the beaker back.

'No, it is to keep for you.'

We kiss again but, before anything else can happen, George's head appears over the dune.

'You Finnish?' he says laughing.

We walk along the strand.

'Our address.'

'Oh yes,' says George.

Helvi writes their addresses on a piece of paper and hands it to George.

'For film,' she says

'I write to you,' says George

'What is film about?' says Aino.

George hesitates. He's stuck or else he doesn't want to stretch his brain now that he has already got what he was after.

'It's about a married man,' I say, 'who makes love to other women.'

'Ah yes.' Aino's eyes light up. 'And we may be the other women.'

'Perhaps,' I say

'A story of love?'

'Oh yes, during a revolution.' I don't know why I say revolution. Maybe it sounds romantic. I'm trying to make George into some romantic figure like Doctor Zhivago and I look across at him, at his condoms bulging in his pocket and his big Doc Martens and, except for the moustache, I know I'm pushing it.

George is edgy. He's lost interest. He wants to get away. He wants new territory.

We say goodbye to Aino and Helvi who head off further up the beach perhaps to collect more shells or things washed up by the sea, little shards of georges or séamuses that they can bring home in their bags as souvenirs. They become smaller and smaller as they move away, becoming like little dots, becoming like the little stones or shells that earlier they themselves were collecting. Maybe something larger will come along out of a great cloud or from the ocean deep and collect *them*. They walk on, disappearing ultimately, sucked into nothingness by the wide expanse.

I steal a side look at George. His brow is furrowed now; his lips are puckered; thoughts are forming. 'I'm going to tell you something, Franky ...' He pauses. 'You never know, you never really know what goes on in a woman's head.'

'How do you mean, George?'

Tears well in his eyes. Where were they at Freddy's funeral, I wonder, those tears?

'They're not foolproof you know.'

'Women?' I say.

'No, fuck sake. Johnnies. They don't always work.'

The bus trudges through misty rain. Little bulbs lighting enhance the darkness outside the glass. *Coming home*. To George's house. I feel under a compliment. Thing are not the same anymore between us; there's a cooling off since the outing in the car, since I mentioned about the circumstances of Freddy's death. I keep thinking about George, how he operates, how he gets the women. George the opportunist, the spoofer. Is that the way of it? Is that the way to go? Spoof, pretend? Win them to a lie? But that episode on the strand, to George, it was just a puff of wind, a bit of fluff blowing in from the sea, that one forgets about as quickly as not – George seems to be good on that score: forgetting. But what did I do during it all? Nothing; smothered as I was in the blubber of a chuckling voluptuary, waiting for him to *finish*. I mean what *could* I do? I was a married man, no matter what George thought; it had to count for something. And the girl: she was a charitable soul really who gave me her blue beaker, which I hold in my hand now, like the flotsam of a dream.

But I don't have to worry unduly about George. He's away a lot, and with Noreen in hospital, it means I have the house to myself a fair bit. But I am apprehensive of being so close to 'home.' It's inevitable I'll meet them, the two next door, bump into them no doubt. (Hard to avoid Myrtle's bumps).

I could of course go back to Ivy Cottage. I could try to break down the walls of loneliness that entrap my father's life but it's too difficult, for the moment at least. I've too many problems of my own for me to be subsumed by his unrelenting night. When I think of all the years I had dedicated to him in Ivy Cottage, I am seized by twinges of self-pity. Besides, Dad is not faring too badly. He's getting his meals up in the Centre now.

Mrs Dempsey arranged it. A place specially run for old folks by some of the women of the avenue giving their services voluntarily. A bus collects him every weekday and drops him home afterwards, so at least he's getting a square meal five days of the week. Mrs Dempsey usually has him in on a Saturday, and that only leaves Sunday when I generally go over to Ivy Cottage and drum something up for him.

I've cooked for George too a couple of times, when he's in that is. I don't mind. It's the least I can do in return for his hospitality. He's no great hand at the cooking, George. Goes for the takeaways, although the two of us have sat down on occasion to roast chicken and spuds, or maybe a bit of grilled fish. But he is always restless and is off as soon as the meal is over, never saying where he is going, and some nights (as I discovered earlier) he doesn't come back at all. One evening when he's rushing out I say to him, 'What about Freddy?' 'What do you mean, what about Freddy?' he says. 'Have you done any thinking about it?' 'I'm in a hurry now.' 'We have to report it,' I say, 'about what happened.' 'Look,' he says, opening the door, 'I'll look after that, okay?'

Tonight, after tidying up in the kitchen, I go into the sitting room and sit on George's sofa, wondering what my next move will be. The two next door seem to be away. No sounds from there for a while, whatever they're up to. I press the TV button: some soap which I turn off as quickly as I had turned it on. Too unsettled to read, I wonder about Sandra. Is she still bopping in the Diamond? The aura is shattered now since seeing her there, and hearing her voice, and this Spikey, what power does he hold over her, and what is his connection with Freddy, and why is George silent on it all? There are terrible things happening, as Mrs Dempsey says. I think of my childhood, that Shangri-La. Sometimes I long to go back there, to try to break through the coded time to get back to the safe time. The safe time ended for me one week before my twelfth birthday. That was the day my mother was killed. She was going to bring me to the cinema, to the pictures as we called them then, to see Elvis playing a straight role as a half-breed in *Flaming Star*. And there was the promise after of a Knickerbocker Glory in the Palm Grove café.

The Indian knows he's going to die when he sees the flaming star. He prepares. He goes to the top of a mountain and lies down and the buzzards devour him. He is usually old, but my mother wasn't old, no more than Elvis. The star came out too early for both of them.

I never saw my mother die. She was crossing the road near our cottage, so I'm told, when a sports car came speeding. I came home from school that day and she was gone. I remember Mrs Dempsey making fresh scones with jam, and when I cried she told me not to cry, that my mammy was taken to heaven. I don't know who decided I should not see her remains. She must've been cut up pretty badly. The only mark to remind me of her that I was allowed to see was the bent bus stop where the car came to a halt.

That's why I never bothered learning to drive, because learning to drive could also mean learning to kill.

The driver of the sports car apparently was some fellow showing off with his girlfriend. There is one phrase I remember: 'flirtatious behaviour', that was how Mrs Dempsey described the way the fellow carried on, but she said no more than that and always changed the subject whenever I tried to talk about it at a later stage. They were trying to shelter me I suppose. Shield me from the pain. So after a while I just stopped enquiring. And, as for my father, he kept it all inside, except for the silent seepage through his eyes.

I like to think that the bus stop was left like that in memory of my mother rather than due to negligence on the part of the bus company. And I looked at it on my way to school and on my way home from school for a long time before it was repaired.

My father broke down after my mother died. I didn't understand it at first. We must have been a sorry sight, the pair of us. How could one so young understand things like breakdown or depression or failing mental faculties? A child doesn't think of a parent in such a context. The neighbours helped out of course, and Mrs Dempsey was always in and out. I vaguely remember some woman, although I can't picture her, who never spoke, coming to help us for a while.

As time went on and people called a little less often I found myself taking on more and more domestic duties. I had to become a father to my father. I had to cook, console – console with my child words – simply in order that he would continue to live. My father was a machine who had entrusted the workings of himself to my mother, and when she died, the keys to work the machine were buried with her. I was left with a motor that I had to kickstart every day. To get him up out of bed in the morning was the hardest thing. I would rail at my father with tears in my eyes. He would just lie there, not asleep, staring at nothing. In desperation once, when hoarse from shouting, I applied Mam's smelling salts to his nose. He didn't get angry. He just pulled himself out of bed with a groan like Frankenstein's monster coming to life. But Dad wasn't a monster and I would've preferred if he'd got angry.

My father grew fond of Paracetemol. He took large quantities of these tablets, not because he had any physical pain, but to try to alleviate the pain of life. One day I found him in the garden shed staring at the jagged edge of a broken bottle which he was holding in his hand.

I went to school. I came home. I cooked. I washed. I sewed. I sewed the ends of my childhood to the bulk of my adolescence. So two phases in a person's life, for me at least, were now reduced to one.

I never knew what *flirtatious* was. I even looked up the word in a dictionary after Mrs Dempsey had used it about the sports car driver. *Frivolous* was one of the synonyms given. I wasn't really clear on the sexual element of the word then, so I latched onto *frivolous,* which I remembered was a word a teacher had used about some idle boy in school who was always gadding about and rarely did his homework.

I saw the frivolous ones coming home from school, hanging around corners for hours on end. That Ida Hourigan was there with the short straight hair when other girls wore pigtails or curls, or delighted in long manes down their backs. She messed around with a group of girls, taunting the boys, making vulgar suggestions even then. She was always on the avenue and I don't know if Myrtle was one of those with her.

I used to hate it when I heard the mothers calling their offspring in for dinner or calling them to do an errand. And I heard their laughter trailing off into the twilight and it filled me with desolation.

That's when I really got into reading. I carried a book with me everywhere. There was a little lending library in the newsagent's shop (you had to pay but it wasn't very much). It wasn't far from the avenue. There weren't many books there to attract a boy of my age. They mainly stocked Mills and Boon romances for the women and Zane Grey westerns for the few men who would bother to browse. But whatever they had by Dickens or Stevenson or Ballantyne, I consumed.

I had fixed times. For example, I'd read a chapter while waiting for potatoes to boil and could get through a few pages in the loo. If the book was a sturdy tome I could balance it on the kitchen sink and read as I washed the plates. It took Myrtle to point out to me later that washing dishes in that way left many stains undetected. But my father never said anything. He never complained. It wasn't stains on plates that worried him.

Reading was great. It took my mind to other worlds while I physically remained in a world of groans and dirty dishes. So many, even though there were only two to wash for – we tended to use a lot of ware and let it accumulate which was in keeping with the couldn't-be-bothered attitude of my father. I started counting how many plates we washed and dried and clattered. I wrote the number down, but after I reached a thousand I stopped. That's when I realised that some things are futile. The banging of plates didn't bother me then, but the sound must have entered my subconscious somehow. It must have been there all the time without my knowing, until Myrtle came along. She brought it out. She banged plates and kettles and

84

doors louder than I ever did. With her it was like a calling never to be at rest. I never chipped china. Myrtle often did despite her kitchen pride. And she didn't care what she damaged when she was angry.

Sometimes people, like artists, will themselves into isolation and expect the world to weep for them. Their work is their spokesperson, the long years of dedicated toil, even though they do not request it, that is what they want to be judged on if at all. My father was a bit like that, but I was too young to understand such things then. For a long time after my mother died, he would sit at the kitchen table for hours on end and cry silently, like a faithful dog whining over the departure of a lost friend. And the idea occurred to me that maybe he was thinking that if he sat there long enough in Mam's kitchen he could will her somehow to return, in spirit at least. The tears would fall onto his plate. The meal which I had prepared would remain uneaten. There was nothing I could do or say. I had not the experience of life or the years to confide in him as an equal. I thought he was resigning himself to die. Who would have believed, looking at him then, that he would still be alive today? I found that the hardest part of all: just sitting there looking at him, unable to do anything. And that's when I'd open a book and read silently, the silent words entering my head, harmonising in some strange way with the silent tears falling from his eyes. I was satisfied that my presence was there for him (in case he would do anything silly), but my mind found solace elsewhere.

My father worked as a gardener for the original owner of the estate where the avenue is now. The manor was known as the colonel's house. Some old English colonel had owned the house and the surrounding land. He was another someone whom I never saw. Perhaps he died before I was born. Perhaps they were his descendants who were running the house when I was a kid. I can't quite remember.

So growing up, I was surrounded by trees and fields with hedgerows. There was no such thing as suburbia in our vocabulary. It was just a simple blend between country and avenue, *rus in urbe,* or rather the other way round; just a follow-through, a gradual increase in the number of homes and people minding their own business (which was always the way with us).

My father was a good gardener, an artist in a way, blending the ornate with the practical, growing Sweet Williams in the company of cabbages, and Dahlias (which he pronounced as dallies) protected from the frost by the same straw as used for his seed potatoes. He preferred apple trees to cherry blossoms. The apple, he argued, provided the ornate in its flower and the practical in its fruit, unlike the cherry blossom which gave no fruit in an unpredictable climate such as ours and which, according to my father, always seemed to be the tail end of someone else's weather. I think my father thought like that about ourselves as well: that we were the tail end of something else.

He taught me the names of plants. He was okay when he was gardening. He was autonomous in a world of verdure, or maybe it was because he knew there was someone there for him at the end of the day. He brought me to the colonel's gardens. He brought me through the maze of yew hedges – *the puzzle*, he called it. 'Life's like that,' he said, 'life's a puzzle.' He taught me about topiary. That's what prompted me to think of him as an artist. He could sculpt birds and animals out of leaves. He showed me the blue of the *myosotis*. 'Forget me not,' he said, and his voice had a pleading tone.

Except when he spoke on plants, my father was a taciturn man. My mother was my father's tongue. She provided him with many prompts when he was speaking; she would complete his words or sentences for him, and I just presumed that this was the normal form of dialogue of married couples. The wife/mother was always the more articulate of the partnership in any of the families that I knew; it was just taken for granted. The woman was the storyteller, the reader of romances. The husband was the physical provider, the caveman who communicated in monosyllabic grunts.

It was when she died that he slowly started to lose his memory. Or maybe it started earlier I don't know, but I never noticed it before then. Once, not long after she died – perhaps it was an early warning sign – my father wandered away from the cottage and headed down the avenue, and I spent half the evening looking for him; and all he said when I found him was that he was looking for the fields. And then he went down to the Diamond.

The Diamond in those days was smaller than it is now, no lounge, just a bar with wooden stools on a concrete floor and flagstones covered in sawdust. My father went there to bemoan the changing ways of the world with some like-minded men, and sometimes he came home with a bottle of lemonade for me. Other times he forgot to come home, and I had to go and get him. I saw grey-haired men with weather-beaten faces and thick moustaches, and I remember the smell of porter and tobacco and the spitting on sawdust, and I witnessed the strange generosity of drunkenness, the pat on the head, the shilling, the voices saying 'grand lad', 'good boy', 'a credit to you'.

It wasn't that my farther drank a lot. He just forgot about time. He forgot about darkness falling or about a schoolboy who had homework to do for school next day. Or maybe he didn't forget any of these things. Maybe these were things he could not face.

Some of my school fellows used to call to the cottage for me to go out to play. A lot of them were the new kids, *the avies.* They would come around with their marbles or chestnuts or footballs. I went out to them sometimes, but my play was always limited. There was always some chore that needed to be done.

It was only much later when my father faltered over the names of his favourite trees and shrubs, that I first realised the vulnerability of memory. He taught me the names and then he forgot the names, and now I have to teach him. But I can't teach him. There is nothing to keep the names in. His mind is like a sieve. I said a name to him one day before deafness set in. 'The wine-coloured tree,' I said, 'the maple.' 'The maple?' *'Acer. Acer palmatum.* Remember you told me its leaves are shaped like hands.' 'Hands?' he said, and he looked at his hands as if not knowing what they were.

But things got worse when he went deaf. Deafness is the ultimate isolation. When he started going deaf he would ask for endless repetitions of what I was saying. I was permanently on playback, and I found the strain hard to bear. Continuous repetitions of words and sentences in increasing volume, apart from taking its toll on my voice, brought a heavy weight to bear on my chest, making me breathless like when I had asthma. So I bought him a notebook with a tunnel on its back where you could slide a pencil in or out. I wrote my answers and stock questions in the notebook, once only, and if my father wanted repetitions, I simply referred to the appropriate page.

I got him to write things down too when he forgot what he wanted to say halfway through a sentence. Sentences were like long journeys for him which, if he did complete, left him mentally winded, and he would be cross and tired for a long while afterwards. He would write the first couple of words of a sentence and then just stare at the page like he stared at the trees he could not name. He would keep looking at his unsteady scrawl as if it belonged to someone else. And then he would look at me imploringly with those watery eyes, and that was the worst part of all.

My communication with my father became briefer and briefer, but it was rarely contentious. (I never understood the generation gap arguments that my school mates spoke of. I never went through an Oedipal stage. How could I?) But it had a spillover effect on how I related to others. In company, initially, I would be reticent, fearing that if I spoke I would have to go into some long rigmarole of explanation of what I meant. And when I did have to speak, I was terse almost to the point of being monosyllabic (polysyllables were for the thinking me). I was just like my dad used to be at the best of times.

I had perfected this laconic style by the time I met Myrtle. So, she was able to do enough talking for both of us. It was okay by me. In the beginning that is.

My father was not a bad man. He didn't always cry either; besides after a while, tears solidify and one gets on with life. One *has* to get on with it. What choice is there? In addition to working for the colonel, he spent most of his free time in our own garden, whose spaciousness I took for granted until I moved into the avenue (suburbia, if it does exist, is a miniaturisation). He was fine when he was outdoors, although I liked to check on him when he went into the shed. He grew ivy on the walls of our cottage, Goldheart, the evergreen or the evergold, and the deciduous Boston ivy which to this day is still a synecdoche of autumn for me with its flame-red colour, making me imagine that the cottage was bleeding. Thus when my father came home one day with an oak carving with the name Ivy Cottage engraved on it, our home was at least accurately if simply named.

Another day – maybe a year or so after my mother died – he surprised me with a parcel wrapped in brown paper. I don't know where he had been, but he was all spruced up in a fresh shirt and Brylcreemed hair, and his gnarled, arthritic hands were spotless (except of course for the unremovable blemish under the nails).

When I opened the parcel I discovered a book called *Gulliver's Travels*. The book had such a wonderful smell, the smell of newness with its crisp pages, and leather binding, waiting like virgin land for me, its first explorer.

'I know you like to read,' he said.

'The gardaí are no bloody good,' says George when I ask him if he went to the station about Freddy.

'You did go?'

'Of course I went, but all they said was they needed proof. They just wrote everything down in a bloody book. They can't prove anything.'

'Did you tell them that Spikey threw the ball up onto the pylon?'

'I told them that.'

'The kids saw him.'

'I know. But that's no good. They said they questioned Spikey and he said that Freddy climbed up the pylon off his own bat.'

'What about the knife? Did you say he had a knife?'

'He was just cleaning his nails with it. He didn't threaten anyone with it. He said that Freddy went up further on the pylon just to show off.'

'You believe Spikey?'

He sighs. 'What a name to pin on a young man.'

'What?' I say.

'Spikey,' he says, 'it's terrible to be lumped with a name like that.'

I can't believe this. He's feeling sorry ... he's actually feeling sorry for this creature.

'What do yo mean, George?'

'Got to go, Franky.'

The house is cold even though I have a coal fire burning in the grate in the sitting room. There is sparse furniture, just the basics, a few presses and lino in the sitting room. You can't heat an empty house. I hear the kids in the avenue being summoned in. I look out the window and watch the autumn slowly giving way, ceding to the next season, waiting hungrily on standby. Few leaves left on the trees now as a drizzly gloom descends. I look around the room. Walls. I feel closed in. Walls that were weeping once. When is Noreen coming home? *Is* Noreen coming home? I forgot to ask George. Would he even know? No sounds from next door.

How did Myrtle and I become an item? George asked me that one evening. There was a sort of teasing in his voice. It was funny I suppose, George asking me that, but it set me thinking back.

The bus stop (my mother's monument) was near our cottage and where Myrtle used to get off the bus on her way home from work. She worked in a department store, in ladies' fashions somewhere in the city. She always looked very smart in elegant clothes which suited whatever season we were in. With her dark hair often tied in a snood and her sallow skin she could have passed for a gypsy or a flamenco dancer. Myrtle only had the hint of plumpness then, something which accentuated her shapeliness and made her attractive. In hindsight I suppose her clothes were really a bit staid, a lot of tweeds, costume suits, bulky tartan skirts, conservative dresses with exaggerated floral displays (something like her taste in wallpaper). But to me in those years it was not out of place and maybe, deep down, it was that very staidness that I craved at the time.

Myrtle smiled at me one day when I was in the garden with my father. I was nineteen then. That was my first contact with Myrtle and she continued to smile at me every time she passed by (I always made a point of being in the garden for the half five bus). I was flattered that such a mature and well-developed woman should take an interest in a youngster who reddened every time she was near. The first time we spoke she was wearing black high heels and a tweed suit and carried a leather handbag. Myrtle told me it was crocodile leather but Mrs Dempsey, who had seen her, swore blind afterwards that it was only imitation leather, that any fool would know by its exaggerated shine. But I paid no heed to what I put down as the pettiness of an elderly woman with nothing better to do.

I was trimming the roses around the pergola, cutting out dead wood.

'They're nice roses,' she said.

I said nothing but snipped a bud and offered it to her.

She lifted the flower to her nose. 'It has a nice scent.'

'It's called *Sympathy*,' I said.

'Thank you, Francis.'

'You know my name?'

'Of course,' she said, 'everybody knows about you.'

It was then I realised how lonely my life had been.

We went to the blackberry field one sunny, late August day. (She had suggested going there for a walk and, as the blackberries were bursting with ripeness that year, I recommended we go pick some). It was a fine stretch of field behind our cottage where houses are now. We were filling a billycan. Myrtle was giggly. She said it was funny that she had been to the blackberry field many times but this was the first time she came to collect blackberries. She climbed on a mound of grass and reached up on her tiptoes and stretched to pick a ripe fruit. The sun caught the shine in her hair, the shape of her breasts through her blouse, the curves of her hips, and illumined a path up her dress to the secret delights of her thighs.

She turned and smiled at me, the smile of one who knows she was being admired. 'I'm stuck,' she said. 'Help me down, Francis,' and she slid down through my arms, so slowly, so sensually, allowing my hands to rub against her breasts and come to rest on the curvature of her hips. She took the slide out of her hair and shook the mop loose like a horse shaking his mane to declare his freedom from a bridle or a bit. Loose and wanton she shook her hair, throwing her head back. She put her index finger in her mouth and sucked it. 'A thorn?' I said, and she took it out slowly to show me there was nothing there. And then she kissed me, guiding my hand to forbidden places.

She called around to the cottage the next day with a blackberry tart which she had just baked. I invited her in and was about to make tea, but she took the teapot from me and insisted on making the tea herself. She became a regular caller after that. She helped with the washing up and the cleaning and the dusting. She started to rearrange things (gradually) in the kitchen, little things like where certain cutlery went. My father became confused. He had trouble finding things at the best of times but now had to ask Myrtle where his porridge bowl was. She lost her patience with him when he repeatedly asked her about the location of the bowl. I accepted it. It was good for us, a bit of order that is. My father needed someone to sharpen him up. But I got exasperated over a tea and milk incident. My father didn't take milk in his tea, not since the War years when he got used to rationing. 'We can all do on less,' he said. Myrtle had the habit of nearly half-filling the teacups with milk before pouring tea into them. I told her several times that my father didn't take milk in his tea but all she said was, 'Codswallop, everybody takes milk in their tea.' For a number of days my father drank no tea at all until one evening, unable to take any more of this cold war, I furtively emptied his milk into my own cup. Myrtle didn't notice or pretended not to notice as I poured the tea.

I was disappointed in my father afterwards as this secret act between us became a regular feature of the tea ceremony whenever Myrtle was around. I wanted him to show a twinkle in his eye or some sign of a little victory on his face or even a hint of gratitude. But he just sat there, beetle-browed and silent, staring into space.

Myrtle's domestic interest extended from the kitchen to the cottage in general. She arrived with paint one day and painted the front door and window frames mauve. She never asked us about the colour. I suppose if, in her eyes, we couldn't make a cup of tea, she was hardly going to consult us about colour schemes. We didn't mind. It was great to have a woman in the house. At least I didn't mind. My father said nothing.

One day Myrtle asked me if I knew who the fellow was who drove the car that killed my mother. I said I never saw the fellow, and that was when I heard her whistling for the first time.

When she told me she was pregnant, she said, 'What are you going to do about it?'

Her tone was cold. She was no longer the accommodating, smiling Myrtle of the blackberry field. She just called over to me one day and said it. Knocked on my door and said straight out, 'You never used a johnny.'

Use a johnny? It was strange to hear a girl express such a word. I had never even seen a johnny, much less use one.

'It was only once,' I said.

'Once is enough. Are you going to do the honourable thing now, Francis?'

The marriage was a lightning affair. Myrtle and Ida were like army generals rasping orders to left and right, conducting a swift military campaign. Unless ordered to do something, my father and I were left standing like bemused onlookers.

I remember saying to Ida, 'Are you the bridesmaid?' She looked at me with that examining look which I have got to know more than once since. A look that runs you up and down, trying to unnerve you, and seems to always rest on your crotch, trying to force you to look down to see if your fly is open or maybe something worse.

'Bridesmaid?' she said. 'Ha. If I'm the bridesmaid, you're the gobshite.'

I remember the flowers in the church. Mrs Dempsey's chrysanthemums which are my least favourite and which were the flowers for ordinary autumn Sundays (my father or I had no say in the matter). I remember the reception in the Diamond extension which is called the No Ice because when the notice for the extension was put up the letter T was whipped, and since then people always referred to the extension which also houses the off-licence as the No Ice. I remember the wedding cake, a one tier affair. One felt it was a

94

token merely to fulfil obligations. I found that strange even then because Myrtle had boasted about her cooking and baking abilities. It just seemed odd that she would accept a cake so small. And the number of guests – mainly from the avenue – she kept to a minimum.

Myrtle's father, a small man with eyebrows so bushy they could accommodate rebels, showed positive delight in giving the bride away. I hardly knew the man. Myrtle wasn't interested in introducing him to me. At the reception I met him in the *Gents* and he said to me, 'Thanks be to Jaysus she's off my hands, that's all I'll say to you, sonny boy,' and I wasn't even sure if he knew my name.

All this whizzed past me like future video cassettes on fast forward. And the dancing: the jive or waltz or whatever they were, I couldn't do, and I was whirled around like a circus animal until all the world was dizziness.

After our marriage we moved into Ivy Cottage. It didn't take long, a couple of months at the most, for Myrtle to tire of my father. His silences, his grubby hands, his weepiness, all irritated her. She tried whenever possible to banish him from her presence. She had already banished him from the master bedroom and the marriage bed where my mother had conceived me. It now became our matrimonial suite (of sorts) and my father was relegated to my room and my single bed. He didn't utter a word of protest. He just moved his things in silence like air that blows through a door or a window just causing a slight shudder. She forced him to stay outside *her* kitchen until meals were ready, and sometimes she arranged it so that my father dined at different times to us.

I didn't defend my father against Myrtle's onslaughts. The truth is I was afraid she would withdraw her 'favours' which even at this early stage she was beginning to ration. Like a lot of other people she thought that my father was dying. 'A man can only take so much grief,' Mrs Dempsey said, and it was the only time I remember Myrtle concurring with her. My new bride thought my father would die quickly and leave the cottage to the two of us. But depression is a deceptive thing and it doesn't necessarily shorten one's life. To Myrtle, my father was an inconvenience and my wife hated inconveniences.

Eventually despairing of any hope of his early departure from this world, she said, 'I can't stand that pathetic man. If he won't go, we'll have to get a house.'

I wanted to retort to Myrtle that she was going too far this time, that she couldn't put a man out of his own home, but all I came out with was, 'You know he won't go.'

And that's when she went to Ida's.

I called around to Ida's place several times. 'I want to see my wife,' I would say to Ida who would only half open the door. 'You can't see her,' she would reply. 'She will se you when she's good and ready and not before that? 'What do you mean good and ready?' I would say, but she would close the door on my face. I was disappointed with Myrtle. I couldn't believe that she wouldn't come out and at least talk to her husband.

I spent those months – which seemed like years – without Myrtle in a befuddled state. Going and coming from work, helping my father with chores, spending long, solitary evenings staring out windows, with no one to confide in, and wondering at times had I really got married or was it all some strange dream. When she eventually returned, having announced the miscarriage, she proclaimed as if she'd never been away, 'Number forty eight is up for sale on the avenue.'

'Is that all you can say?' I said, 'after going away on me like that.'

'Don't you start,' she said. 'You've no idea what a woman goes through. You've no idea what it's like to lose a baby.'

'My father helped out with the money,' I said.

I looked across at my father. He was sitting at the table stirring his tea, not hearing a word.

'After all we did for him, it's the least he can do for us,' she said.

It was much later I found out she had told Ida and possibly half the avenue that she had contributed the larger part of the down payment, and that it was her money and hands that had refurnished and redecorated the house.

'Does it have to be this house?' I said.

'It's the only one available.'

'No, it's not. There's one around the back,' I said for I had seen a *For Sale* sign on another house at the back of the avenue.

'That's already sold,' she said.

When Myrtle first started to put on weight, I never said anything. But later in the marriage when I tackled her on her chocolate, crisp and Guinness bingeing, she said, 'Ida doesn't mind.' 'What do you mean, *Ida doesn't mind*?' I said. 'What's Ida got to do with your weight?' She was taken aback. 'She accepts me the way I am.' 'And what way is that?' I said, and Myrtle tried to silence me by switching on the vacuum cleaner.

Normally a vacuum cleaner is a successful instrument in terminating arguments between Myrtle and me, but I was tired of being constantly dismissed, of being fobbed off by a machine. I went over to the socket and pulled out the plug.

'What are you doing?' she screamed.

'I asked you a question,' I said.

'Put that plug back in.' She was beginning to froth but I stood my ground.

'Why me, Myrtle? You don't love me.'

'You better get out of this house.'

'You probably never did except that once in the blackberry field and that was probably just a trick.'

'A trick?'

'Yeah. A ruse to get me hitched, and now you're trying to throw me out of my own house.'

'You don't deserve a house.'

'It was always that way,' I say, 'wasn't it Myrtle, between Ida and you?'

I'm going through the microfiche checking something for a borrower when Dad taps me on the arm with his notebook. I open the appropriate page. HOW ARE YOU DAD? DID YOU LOCK THE FRONT DOOR AFTER YOU? The page is a bit crinkled and dog-eared now from use.

Dad refuses to look at the page. He brushes the notebook aside with his hand. He is agitated. 'The cottage was robbed,' he says.

'Hang on, Dad.' I go over to Michael who is sorting books on a trolley.

'I've to do something,' I say. 'Will you keep an eye on things?'

'Su ... sure Francis,' says Michael with his little stammer. 'Ho ... how's the chin?'

'Getting better,' I say. I had told Michael I had a little accident, didn't elaborate.

'I won't be too long.'

I have my hand on Dad's shoulder as we walk towards his cottage at the end of the avenue. I want to console him in some way, but how do you console an old, deaf man who cries in public. It's embarrassing. My father cried too much for me to feel strong in the world. I remember one summer when everyone was complaining about the rain. Everyday it came down for weeks, not in a great downpour, but in a slow endless drizzle, and my father said he hoped it would never stop because he didn't want to be left alone with his sadness.

Mrs Dempsey is standing at the wrought iron gate when we arrive, hands folded over her brown bib. 'It's a disgrace Francis, what they did,' and then when I get close up she exclaims, 'Jesus Mary and Joseph, what happened to your chin?'

'It's all right now.'

'That Myrtle one,' she mutters, perhaps thinking also of my knee 'accident'. She was always suspicious of Myrtle even though I never told her the truth of that story. 'Did you get someone to look at it?' she enquires solicitously.

'I did, Mrs Dempsey,' I say impatiently, 'now will you tell me what happened?'

'They've no shame. An old man like that.' She turns to my father. 'Are you all right, Sam?' She speaks the words loudly, spelling them out with her lips.

'What happened?' I repeat.

'They took advantage of him. He was cutting his hedge when two of them came along. I saw them from my window. I knew what they were up to. I rang the gardaí, but they were too fast for them.'

'Who were they?'

'A young fella and a young one.'

'Could you make them out'?

'Oh God.' Mrs Dempsey clasps her hands together as if invoking the divine for assistance. 'You couldn't tell who they were, not with their helmets on and your one even had her what do you call it? pulled down.'

'Her visor?' I say.

'That's it. For a minute I thought she looked like Dorothy Murphy's young one, but with the way everything happened so fast I couldn't be sure. But I knew by the get up of them, by their leather jackets and chains and all that they were cider-drinkers. The fella talks to your father at the hedge not realising he is deaf and Sam, God love him, grateful for a bit of company smiles up at him ...' She looks compassionately at my father who all the time is standing in his cap and overcoat like a grey statue by my side '... while your one slips in behind his back through the open door.'

'On the latch?' I say.

'What?'

'The door, was it on the latch?

'Yes. The innocent.'

'On the latch, Dad,' I say loudly turning to my father. 'How many times have I ...?'

'What's that?' Dad says with a shake in his head.

'He can't hear you, Francis.'

'I know. I know,' I say irritably, too frustrated to write anything down.

'She comes out of the cottage carrying what looks like a jewellery box. I shout to Sam and go out as fast as me hip will allow me, but they push me down on the path as they run past. They get up on this big motorbike and off they go with your brazen one on the back holding the box.'

'Were you hurt, Mrs Dempsey?'

'No no. Your father, God be good to him, comes over to me and helps me up. Me hip is plastic you know, Francis. I was all right, but your misfortunate father ...'

'The box, was it black velvet?'

'It *was* black.'

'My mother's.'

Mrs Dempsey sighs. 'All gone now for cider.'

I am still outside talking to Mrs Dempsey when George drives along by the cottages. I hail him down. We explain what happened. We get into the car. Mrs Dempsey sits in the back seat. Dad is reluctant to get into the car. He throws a disapproving look at George as if there is something between them, something unpleasant unknown to me. This is the first time I have witnessed George and my father together. George looks uncomfortable. He keeps his head lowered. He presses the cigarette lighter on the dash and when it pops out he presses it again. Mrs Dempsey tries to coax my father into the car. 'Forget the past, Sam,' she says out loud, hoping that he can hear, but my father stands his ground.

I grab Dad's notebook and write, WHAT IS IT DAD? WE'RE GOING TO LOOK FOR THE THIEVES WHO ROBBED YOU.'

My father shakes his head.

'Not in his car,' he says turning back towards his cottage.

I sit in the front seat. George is driving fast as if he wants to get the journey over with. That's unusual for George. Normally he drives too slowly when he's sober and too fast when he's drunk. He doesn't look happy.

We circle around the avenue. Kids are playing. I see John Paul and Tomo kicking a ball. I ask George to stop the car. George frowns but complies. I ask the boys if they saw a motorbike with a man and a girl on it. They say no motorbike came up the avenue. George doesn't look at the boys. He revs the car impatiently. We drive on around the estate. The street lamps are just coming on, showing an orange glow before shining fully with white light.

'A disgrace,' Mrs Dempsey says from the back seat, 'the way they treat old people. They forget they'll be old themselves someday. Imagine your own home is not safe any more.'

'We'll go down to the garda station, George,' I say.

He looks alarmed. 'What? Is there any point?'

'Should I tell Father Mack?' asks Mrs Dempsey.

Neither of us answers her.

'I have to report it, George.'

'I'll drop you off,' he says coolly looking at his watch.

The same sergeant, to whom I'd reported about the heroin in the football, takes down my statement. As he writes I notice that, as well as being ruddy-complexioned, he's also grossly overweight and I wonder how in his condition he would catch a criminal if he had to run after one. I talk about my father and the robbery. I don't say anything about being assaulted. I'm afraid of incriminations, afraid of the myth makers. I mention George Browne being down about Freddy.

'George?' the sergeant says.

'Browne,' I say.

'I know,' he says. 'Do you really think George would come down here?'

'Can you check the book?' I say.

'If it makes you happy,' he says. 'What date?'

I give the sergeant a number of possible dates. He flicks through the pages of the book.

'There is no record of any statement by George Browne.'

I feel uncomfortable back in George's place. I think George wants me out of his house.

'You can stay as long as you like,' he says. 'It's just that I'll be away for a while.'

I look at George. I want to talk to him about what the sergeant said.

'George,' I say.

'I'm going out to the garden for a smoke,' he says.

'The garden?'

'Yeah. Do you mind?'

There is pique in his voice.

'Of course not, George.'

It is only when he slams the door, I realise that George has stopped calling me by my name.

I'm back in Ivy Cottage in my old room where you would've found me in the pre-Myrtle days. I'm not intending to stay permanently, mind, just long enough to take a breather from George. 'I went,' he said when I eventually got around to asking him about the garda station. 'It's Caffrey didn't record it.' And that's all I could get out of him, and I was surprised at his knowing the sergeant's name.

Dad looks even more worried now than when he was robbed. He is alert. He sits vigilantly on guard at the front window. Nothing like a little danger to quicken the senses when bulldozers are outside your front door. My father won't budge. No one is going to take his home. He owns a freehold as do all the other residents. The builders want to extend the avenue. They see the big gardens attached to the little cottages. They see potential; they smell profit. They could fit a row of apartments where one cottage stood.

They have already offered my father and the other residents alternative accommodation in modern bungalows at the end of the avenue. Dad shakes his head. He does not want a bungalow with an imitation fire to stare at for the rest of his days, a symbol of false nostalgia, a house without a hearth.

The cottage is the heart of him. He often sits in silence in his parlour looking at the wedding photograph of himself and his wife, my mother, on the mantelpiece over the fire. He is clean-shaven in the photograph, showing a square jaw and a deep-channelled philtrum (prior to its hirsute insulation). His dark hair has a parting on the right and his front teeth have a gap like they say of a singer. I have vague memories of his singing old John McCormack or Percy French melodies. A fine tenor voice, someone said – it must have been Mrs Dempsey – but all

103

that was before my mother died. In the photograph he stands broad-shouldered and hopeful, yet slightly vulnerable-looking, as he stares out at the world. He holds the gloved hand of my mother firmly but not too tightly, like two hands linked to steer a clear course straight ahead. They are smiling through the snow of confetti that rests gently on their hair and shoulders. He is aware of the curls of my mother's brown hair; the intricate embroidery on her dress; the bouquet of flowers camouflaging her breasts. The flowers are roses with sprays of gypsophila. I can't tell the colour of the roses – a disadvantage of black and white.

I think of all the slow hours of painstaking preparation that went into that moment, that noontime of their lives rendered eternal by a camera, and I try to examine their eyes for any intimation, for any prior knowledge that they might have had of future tragedy. But there is none except for that little vulnerability, a sort of shyness as they stand there with their backs to the wall of a church. They stand almost shoulder to shoulder, my mother's shoulder just slightly below my father's – for my father is not a tall man. Both are looking at the camera for a moment in past time captured in a rectangular frame for ever. One wants to look beyond the rectangle, to peep inside the corners for an enlargement of their lives, to introduce sound to bring the moment to life, trace it forward with the benefit of hindsight and let lives be lived again with no deaths, safely secured in celluloid which can be played and replayed over and over, fastforwarding and rewinding, without ever having to say there is an end.

To the right of the wedding photograph is a photo of me as a baby of twelve months. I am typically soft and pudgy as I sit with one leg tucked under the other with little sandals and a baby suit, and I am propped up by cushions on a wickerwork chair. I have a squint in the lazy left eye (my kind eye) and blond hair shining with little curls hanging loosely at the back in a sort of studied carelessness characteristic of my mother's style. She went to great pains to be neat. She would spend an age combing her hair and later combing mine and then give my quiff a little tussle as if she wanted a dishevelled look – almost it would seem as if she were a lover of anarchy, as if she were someone who wanted to disturb the prim order of things, but always at the same time seeing the art underneath.

When my father looks at these photographs, I realise that the spirit of all that is him rests there. His wife and himself and his baby captured for eternity in beauty and youth and vigour and surrounded by the warmth of the fire with the logs that he himself had cut. He was the man, the provider. This was his cave, and his reality were these images like the shadows on the cave wall. To remove him from there would be to throw him into a wilderness where beasts of darkness would extract his heart.

The sheriff's men arrive with a court order. I hear the creaking gate and their shoes crunching the desiccated leaves on the path. I look at my father at the window, seeing not hearing. There are no tears in his eyes. He is not the pathetic, weeping man referred to by Myrtle. Not now. There is fire in him. I realise now my father's tears all the years were not signs of weakness at all but simply demonstrations of sorrow, of the pain of loss. My father is strong.

The cottagers stand together. They arm themselves with sticks and shovels. Primitively, the media will say, criminal, pathetically perhaps, but I know the heart-rending dignity of these people. They are prepared to take on the law. They are prepared to question the letter of the law.

I slip in and out of the cottage as unobtrusively as I can, leaving a little earlier for work, returning a little later under the shroud of darkness. It's like I'm leaving and returning to a place of siege every day. My father stays put. He'll not venture out. 'Rubble,' he says. That's what he would return to if they got him out. I bring him food. I cook for him. I sleep or rather rest in my old bed. Like old times almost. There is a garda presence, twenty four hours. At night I watch the silver on their uniforms shining under lamplight. And the big yellow bulldozers with their huge jaws waiting.

A politician calls on my father – a permanently smiling fellow in a blue suit and shirt with a red tie. He offers to furnish the new bungalow if Dad agrees to move out. And of course the word progress is bandied about and used to imply inevitability. 'That's progress,' the politician says, as if all argument is meant to end there.

My father's mind, like Irish weather, can have its moments of clarity. Thus it is now. It is as if he is being summoned by some spirit, perhaps my mother's, or perhaps by a secret inner strength of his own. Staring at a broken glass bottle or wandering off on one's own doesn't prove anything. (I remember him as a kid repairing the pergola during a storm, undaunted by the thunder or lightning flashes).

But when in the raw hours of a Monday morning the *bulldozer* crushes the pergola, my father cannot repair it. The bulldozer levels his garden. He watches wordlessly from his window. The noise of the machine, which irritates me of course, doesn't bother him. To my father the bulldozer is a silent leviathan, a destroyer of art.

The other residents, including Mrs Dempsey, capitulate. 'If we don't move now,' says Mrs Dempsey, 'they'll bulldoze our cottages and we in them. Sam, Sam.' She looks at him worriedly. 'Explain to your father, Francis.'

The politician calls again. I stand beside my father. I proffer the notebook. The politician communicates to my father about the modernity of the new bungalows, of the larger kitchens, of the master bedroom *en suite*.

'*En suite*?' says my father.

The politician writes with Dad looking over his shoulder, with Dad looking more in the world than I ever witnessed before.

'A shower unit and ...'

My father snatches the pencil from the politician's hand.

'How much did they pay you?'

'Who?'

'The land is rezoned,' my father says. 'You did that.'

I stay up with my father that night. We light a log fire in the parlour and sit, as we so often had done in the past, on the two old armchairs with their frayed dralon and battered cushions, quite content with wordlessness. It is not a real silence for we can hear our own breathing and the crackle of the fire, yet it is a state that Myrtle could never have endured or understood. He touches my chin tenderly for a moment with his finger. 'At least it's healing,' he says 'wherever you picked that up.' 'It's nothing, Dad. It was just ...' and I'm thinking of reaching for the notebook, but I say to myself, Oh why bother? To explain what happened in writing would be too complicated and besides, would only add to his worries. He doesn't press me on the matter and we sit watching the flames, feeling the warmth, keeping the late autumn chill out of our bones. My father ups and goes to his little mahogany drinks cabinet and, with that familiar shake in his hand, pours Bushmill's whiskey into two of my mother's lead crystal glasses. He sits beside me. 'Cheers, Dad.' He clinks my glass and I hold it up to the fire's flame and admire the golden glow.

I fall into a doze. When I awake the embers of the fire have died. There is a blanket around me and the photographs on the mantelpiece are missing. My father has gone.

George has collected Noreen from hospital. He carries her – perhaps in the same way he delivers his condom machines – like a parcel up the stairs. He nods to me. I'm back in the Brownes' since the demolition of Dad's cottage. Dad won't speak since he went off that night. He just stands at the front window of the new bungalow watching bulldozers tearing out his heart. It's too much. But George isn't a whole lot better in the word department, and yet the nod may mean he's forgotten our erstwhile coolness. I'm fumbling, clearing the way, opening the wrong bedroom door, trying to be of some assistance, but George doesn't need me. I'm in his way. He dislodges Noreen on a bed in a backroom and, without exchanging a word with her or myself, goes out the front door and drives away.

'Can I do anything for you?' I say to Noreen, feeling embarrassed, feeling I'm in the middle of something I shouldn't be in.

'Maybe you could pull the sheets back so I can get in.'

She puts a matchstick-like arm on my shoulder and I lift her, touching the wool of her dressing gown as I pull the bedcovers back.

'There's no point in getting dressed, George says, when you are simply moving from one bed to another.' She is light, like a little girl except for the wrinkles and veins in her pale skin. There are beads of sweat on her forehead. I prop two pillows behind her back.

'My overnight bag,' she says, 'he wouldn't even bring that up.'

'I'll get it,' I say, glad of the opportunity to have something specific to do.

I go downstairs and return with a blue Adidas sports bag.

'Is this it?'

'Yes,' she says, and I think of the irony of the sports bag as I place it on the floor near her bed.

'I want it closer.' She reaches out and drags the bag nearer to her across a worn piece of carpet where perhaps bags or things were dragged before. It's a mustard-coloured carpet with particles of dust and debris ingrained into it, which have made it black at the edges near the flaking skirting board.

'Thank you, Francis,' she says, taking out some medicines and a little transistor radio. She looks at me. 'I'm really sorry about Freddy.' She sighs. 'It's the past taking revenge.'

'How do you mean?'

'You don't remember me?'

'Remember you?'

'Further back?'

'I remember you vaguely. Your mother used to make the Christmas puddings for the cottagers, didn't she?'

'That's right.'

'I had to collect one once. I think I probably saw you then.'

'Ah.' She sighs again. 'A different girl.'

'I can't put a face on you but I remember all the puddings hanging in calico cloth in the kitchen.'

'That's all you remember?'

'Why?

She pats down the bedclothes. 'No why really. Sometimes when you're on medication you imagine all sorts of things.'

'You heard about me, recently I mean?'

'Philomena Dempsey told me. I was sorry to hear that, Francis. If there's anything ... you know?'

'Thanks.'

'Ha, what can I do? George doesn't tell me anything. The way that woman gets around.'

'Who?'

'Philomena, and look at me not near her age.'

I glance at my watch. 'I should go. I think George wants me out.'

109

'Don't mind him.'

'I don't like wearing out a welcome.'

'He's just afraid of what I might tell you. Anyway, he'll be away for a while.'

She smiles and breathes in, her mouth like a suction hoovering up air. 'Maybe he won't come back at all.'

I wait for her to elaborate about herself and George, but nothing is forthcoming. I think of Noreen's sadness and my father's, and the difference is not in the words so much (it would be an unfair comparison in that area as my father uses so few words), as in the manner of expression and the tone of voice. Noreen's words seem separate from her physical self. The depression is not visible in her eyes as it is with my father. All I can see in her eyes is a dullness (even when she smiles), an apathy as if she is beyond tears. My father never got to that stage, the stage of being beyond feeling.

'You stay as long as you like until you get yourself sorted out. Ha, did I say that? Did I say sorted out? It's the medication talking. No one ever gets sorted out.'

'Can I get you something?'

'Philomena said she'd call.' She presses my hand and smiles faintly. 'Well, maybe a cup of tea would be nice.'

I hear her wheezing as I balance the tea tray on her lap.

'We've both been through the mill, haven't we Francis?'

Tears suddenly well up in my eyes. Out of nowhere, without warning. Words are triggers.

'It's all right, Francis,' she says noticing. 'Sit beside me.' She squeezes her bony hand into mine, brushing lightly across my crotch. 'Everyone has a right to cry in this big weeping club.'

'I should be consoling you,' I say, releasing her hand.

'We all have to lie in the bed we make for ourselves.' She smiles. 'You see, I'm lying in *my* bed.'

'Take it on the chin,' I say, feeling a wound healed now.

She sits up to finish her tea, which nearly tumbles, only for my holding the tray steady. She neatly cuts the crusts off the toast. 'I can't swallow too well,' she says. When she has finished eating, she hands me the tray. 'That was nice, Francis. Thank you. Just leave it by the window. Perhaps you could get my book while you're over there. It's in the drawer in the little table.'

I go to the little table by the window, welcoming the lull that distancing allows. Was the touch accidental? I hear the sound of a motor mower as I place the tray down. The sun is shining outside. I see Ida mowing *my* lawn with the mower my father gave me when Myrtle and I first moved in to the house. How easy it is to claim things.

It is late in the season for cutting a lawn. The mildness has made the grass grow. The motor snarls as Ida hacks away the sporadic tufts peeping through the carpet of leaves. She mows in short fitful starts without rhythm, which causes the engine to cut out, and I can see the foul language written on her lips as she pulls the cord to start up again, and she continues mangling little clumps, marking the lawn with indentations. She is dressed in a denim jacket and jeans with a deliberate cut in the knee trying as always to ape the fashions of the young. A smoking cheroot hangs from her mouth. Myrtle is stooped over the flower border near the frosted remains of *Love Lies Bleeding* and is trimming the grass edges with a shears. Unused to such work (which I considered basic despite my bad knee), she rises and holds her back with her left hand. Ida discards her cheroot into the flower border and goes to rub Myrtle's back. She takes the shears from her. Myrtle goes indoors. Ida looks up and sees me at the window. She opens the shears wide pointing it at me and, clenching her teeth, snaps the blades shut.

'Is it someone mowing?' Noreen says. 'There's always some noise around here. It's when you're lying on your back you hear everything, you know?'

'It's just our neighbours,' I say.

'Ha,' she says.

She is waiting, silent, wondering will I talk about Myrtle, but I say nothing. What is there to say? I look at the book. It's Sartre's *The Age of Reason,* an old Penguin paperback with yellowing pages and a picture of *Guernica* on the cover, price four shillings and six pence.

'George doesn't like me reading,' Noreen says, taking the book. 'It irritates him. Sometimes I have to hide the books.'

'That's not exactly cheerful reading,' I say.

'No, but it's true. Can I tell you about a scene I read? It might offend you.'

'It's okay.'

She flicks though the pages. 'Now where was it? I should have underlined the passage. We forget things if we don't mark them and we sometimes wonder if we really did think what we thought in the first place. Did you ever feel like that Francis?'

'Often.'

'I remember now, it's where Marcelle – that's Mathieu's girlfriend who is ill – coughs up mucus ... You don't mind my saying this?'

'No.'

'Well, she coughs up mucus and she looks at it slowly sliding down the drain of her sink. And she says *c'est la vie,* or rather Sartre says it through her, and it's true, it's life, that mucus sliding down the drain is life, it's the world we live in.'

I am thinking of the image, thinking of a woman speaking like that, thinking of her authentic articulation of the uvular r.

'Any denial of that is a lie. Our existence is really a vile thing. We try to pretend otherwise.'

I look at Noreen and I wonder if it is the type of book she reads or the long convalescence in hospital that has made her so morose. Or was she always like that, or was it George? Did George make her like that, or did she have some hand in fashioning George the way he is?

But when Noreen puts her hand into her overnight bag and lifts a sputum cup to her lips, I know why she quoted Sartre.

I am standing on the site where Ivy Cottage had stood. I measure out the area roughly with long strides. How small it looks now – where it had been. The empty space, and yet not empty, the feeling, the knowing that it is not a void, that something once had filled that space and something remains. How easy it is to erase families from the slate of existence. How easy to pretend they were never there.

The builders are busy clearing rubble. All the stones and bricks and mortar and even a piece of my bedroom wall with a remnant of sky-blue wallpaper still clinging to it, all being made ready for the rubbish tip. And I am relieved my father is not present to witness this desolation close up, for he would surely think he was reliving the Blitz. 'This is a hard hat only site,' a guy in a pinstriped suit says to me.

It's a fine day – cold but dry – as I decide to forego the bus and walk the twenty minute walk to the library to clear my head. Funny, I have a library but no house or perhaps a house of books. Sometimes as I lie in bed at night in Freddy's room (I'm back. I accepted Noreen's invitation, where else could I go?), I think that there is no escape from the avenue. I am hermetically sealed. I have signed my fate. The avenue will fashion me into its own image, whatever that image may be, and I will be sculpted into a paralysis like one of those Greek statues in the colonel's gardens with cavities for eyes and arms cut off at the elbow.

Michael lives near the library, up in the grove. He's happy. He has just got engaged. He says he has found the right girl at last and is saving to get married.

I am looking up a volume on tuberculosis when Michael arrives with the post and a book under his oxter. I turn my head

113

to catch the title, *The Nature of the Second Sex.* He's humming, *Love me do* and I think of the Beatles' music calibrating the youth of another generation. He looks over my shoulder at what I'm reading.

'Fi ... first identified in eighteen eighty two,' he says.

'What?'

'TB. It's on the way back.'

'You're cheerful.'

'There's a letter for you.'

I put the book down and take the letter from Michael. It's from Myrtle or rather from Myrtle's solicitor, newly-acquired, a Ms Goodbody. A letter informing me that if I appear at my own residence again I will be taken to court where a barring order will be issued against me on the grounds of threatening and violent behaviour towards her client, the occupant of the residence, and that the said behaviour was witnessed.

'Ar ... are you all right, Francis?' says Michael.

'I'm fine.'

'It's just your fa ... face ...'

'What?'

'You've gone white.'

'I said I was fine.'

Michael looks at the letter in my hand.

'From a Goodbody,' I mumble half to myself.

'A good buddy?' says Michael.

'That's right,' I say.

I go to the high window. My view is different to what the colonel's would have been. The colonel would have seen perhaps something like a Capability Browne landscape or perhaps something like the landscape on the cover of my paperback edition of *Tom Jones,* which rests on my desk awaiting rereading. It shows a painting of *Westcombe House* by George Lambent, a great vista of dense trees and fields and rivers at different levels fading into the horizon, suggesting an ordered but untamed world, a world to which, like Tom Jones, one could flee and hide away.

My vista, however, when I look out the high window is of grey roofs of houses keeping lids on worlds, keeping things boiling underneath, and chimneys and TV aerials, sparse enough now as most people have the signals piped. I see Spikey coasting along on his motorbike. He sees me and gives me the two finger sign. Then he stops the bike and, as if remembering, takes his knife out from inside his leather jacket. He starts cleaning his fingernails with its tip while giving that Richard Widmark wacko laugh, which I can't hear but which I can see, with its demonic look and curled-up lip. And when the sun catches the steel shining in Spikey's hand, I suddenly think of Ida Hourigan, the would-be peotomist, brandishing her scissors or threatening with my garden shears.

I am about to reread the letter, trying to force myself to be calm, when Michael calls me from downstairs.

'It's your dad.'

My father is looking up at the high stuccoed ceiling, coyly admiring the huge chandeliers which were left with the house, and the great oak beams, and he's thinking perhaps that they don't put that thickness of wood into houses nowadays.

I open the notebook: HOW ARE YOU DAD? DID YOU LOCK THE FRONT DOOR AFTER YOU?

'I locked it after the horse bolted,' he says snappily, still thinking of the old cottage and the robbery.

I add to the note: WHY DID YOU NOT COME TO THE GARDA STATION WITH ME?

My father looks at the page. I don't think he understands.

'George,' I say, forgetting to write.

'The car,' he says, shaking his head in dismay.

Someone hands me a book to stamp a return date.

Dad returns his cap to his head and, repeatedly tapping the annular finger of his left hand with the index finger of his right, slouches away.

I lock the door of the library securely. I double check. Some of the book borrowers had talked of a recent spate of break-ins on the avenue (my dad's obviously was not the only house done). Mrs Dempsey apparently was right in her suspicion because they were all saying it was the cider-drinkers who were to blame.

I pass a billboard advertising bingo with 'top cash prizes'. I walk on past the bus stop, its shelter smashed, the glass in tiny particles strewn across the footpath.

As I step gingerly over the glass, I think this is the spot where my mother was killed, so maybe I should be circumnavigating the route to avoid confronting her memory every day. But that would not be fair to her, for without memory there is only obliteration. Besides, I realise the bus stop is also a monument for a new grave or rather a graveyard now as I look at the stumps of the chestnut trees, jagged like broken pencils, standing in a line.

Machines are drilling holes in the road. JCBs making a patchwork quilt, and another machine is sewing the edges with black threads of tar. A dead squirrel on the road has been pushed into a gully. He was probably looking for his home, his *rus in urbe*.

I call to the chemist's shop with Noreen's prescription for her streptomycin. I almost walk past the shop, my mind as it is dwelling on the letter, dwelling in particular on the phrase *violent behaviour*. How easily words, once uttered, can gel. If one expresses an untruth often enough, can it slowly lose some of its untruthfulness? Can it eventually become a truth? Robin Hood, Dick Turpin, Jesse James, Ned Kelly, were they not just common thieves who were bloated with mythology in the

116

mouths of people?

There's a window broken in the chemist's shop. Cardboard and wooden laths board it up.

'It was the syringes they were after,' says the pharmacist, an elderly man with jughandle ears.

I don't know how long George will be away. I don't know how long I can stay with Noreen. As regards Dad, he's losing the grip of things more and more now, especially since his defeat at the Battle of the Cottage. Can't go back, can't go back to that lost time, I keep saying to myself. Got to keep plodding forward. I want my own house back, and from the Browne's house I can keep an eye on things from close quarters.

So I'm sticking with Noreen even though she sometimes makes me feel uncomfortable – I mean coming on strong in her condition – a bit repulsive. But what intrigues me is what she can tell me about George and about Myrtle and about the lost phase in my own life.

It's a sunny evening as I reach the avenue. Kids are playing football as if they have no memory. Back and forward they go with the ball over the old ground. John Paul and Tomo shout, 'Hiya, Franky'. Their voices have a balmy effect on my ears, like a bandage lying gently on a wound. One could almost pretend that the world is normal and that one is happy as one saunters along. A young one on roller blades wearing kneepads floats past me like a wave undulating from one side of the footpath to the other. I see on an end wall. ~~DRUGS FREE ZONE~~ crossed out and UTCDs painted in aerosol beside it, and NIGGER QUEERS, and in smaller writing. BALLCUTERS OUT with one T missing. Just like in the No Ice.

Looks like pushers down the end of the avenue. A little muster wheeling and dealing in the darkness. They scarper behind a hedge when a squadcar passes. A burglar alarm starts to go off. It's coming from the Carpenters' house. The squadcar turns back down the avenue (the pushers scarper again) and speeds beyond the house with the alarm.

I walk past the pylon, past its new fencing built by the

Council. Up towards my house I see Myrtle and Ida walking, carrying big plastic bags. Myrtle is linking Ida as they approach my gate. She is wearing a new mauve coat. They don't look behind; they seem so content, so smug, I want to shout after them. I want to tell them what I think of them but they'd probably have the gardaí on me, and one could not tell what new accusation they would manufacture against me. If Ida were a man I'd have a strong case. I'd have the right to throw both of them out of my house. But as another woman she would be perceived as an innocent confidante, a kind neighbour consoling an abused wife.

I open the front door of the Brownes' house with the key which George had entrusted to me (funny that he never got around to asking for it back). John Paul shouts from across the road, 'You're goin' into the wrong house, Franky; that's Freddy's.'

Memory is not dead.

But going into the wrong house is not uncommon or even considered bizarre on the avenue – Mr what'shisname does it all the time; sometimes the kids have to guide him into his own house. No, not bizarre at all when one considers that each house, except for the odd paint difference, is like a clone of the one beside it with its uniformity of red brick and pebbledash all the way down the avenue. So walking into the wrong house is just put down as a little aberration, a slight forgetfulness, nothing more.

'I have medicine for Freddy's mother,' I say.

John Paul is standing beside an older boy on crutches. The older boy lowers his head when he sees me looking at him and hobbles away.

'Who was your friend?' I say.

'That was Tomo's brother,' says John Paul. 'He doesn't talk to anyone anymore.'

I pour soup from a can into a saucepan and heat it for Noreen. The cupboard is stacked with Campbell soup cans like an Andy Warhol painting. Funny to be empowered in a kitchen

118

at this stage of my life, if one can indulge the heating of soup as empowerment, but I did cook for George.

'Will you have to go back to hospital,' I say as she takes her tablets.

'Hospital? I wasn't in hospital, Francis, except once. It's the sanatorium. George keeps calling it a hospital.'

I look at a woman growing thinner and more feeble before my eyes, becoming less and less visible in the world, slowly disintegrating as insignificantly as an insect, like the moth lying inert and crumbly on the windowsill.

I sit on a chair beside her bed. 'You said George was afraid you'd tell me things,' I say.

'You probably know them all by now.' Her voice sounds weak. She reaches for her glass of 7UP.

'What things?'

'About your mother.'

'I want to know.' I'm talking firmly, commandingly.

'It was the first car George ever bought. He scraped and saved – imagine George saving. He even cut down on drinking until he got that red sports car.'

'He drove a red sports car?'

'Yes.'

'So he ... I mean it couldn't have been ...'

'It was him, Francis.'

'It was him?'

'Yes.'

'The bastard.' I want a cigarette. I take the packet of mints from my pocket and stuff the two that remain into my mouth.

'Francis.' Her voice is faint, other-worldly. 'I'm truly sorry.'

'But why ...?

'I married out of pity, Francis.'

'Pity? What's that got to do with it?' I say cracking the mints prematurely with my teeth. 'What was there to pity in him?'

She muses for a moment. 'His recklessness I suppose. I felt sorry that he wasn't able to control his life. I thought I could help. I thought I could get him to change. He promised he'd give up the drink. But we can't change, Francis. None of us. The spots keep coming back.'

'Why didn't someone tell me?'

'What good would it have done? Would it have brought the dead back?'

'And why are you telling me now?' It's to get back at George, isn't it?'

She sighs. 'I don't know. Maybe it is. Maybe it's not. What's the point anymore?'

'My father knew.'

'He was full of grief.'

'He just said that the driver of the car was sent to jail. I thought that was the end of it. I thought it was some stranger, someone I would never see or have any inclination to see. Did anyone think of me?'

'I tried to help – offered to do a few chores around the cottage you know, but your father dismissed me. You see I was a mirror to his grief. Don't you understand, Francis, every time he saw me, he wept?'

'You were the one?'

'Yes.'

'You never spoke. I thought you were a mute.'

'It was from shock. But you know the thing I'll always remember is the brown paper. It was a windy day the day your mother died and sheets of it were blowing all over the road like leaves. She was bringing the paper home in her shopping bag. It was to cover your new school books. Your father told me that.'

'My father?'

'Yes.'

I turn towards Noreen's window to hide the tears that are welling. Myrtle and Ida have gone from the garden. The last of the leaves on my own shrubs are falling. Corpses. Mam. Brown corpses falling, decomposing into earth.

'And George,' I say with my back to her, 'what did he do?'

'He did nothing. He actually offered money. Ha. He hadn't two pennies to rub together.'

'To think that bastard killed my mother.'

'Not deliberately, Francis.'

'Why are you defending him all of a sudden?'

'I'm not defending him. Far from it'

I bury my face in my hands. My face in my hands. My head in the sand. Buried. All the years. 'God, half my life, where has it gone?' I turn around and shout at her. 'How could ... how could he ... all the time going around buddy buddy, and not say anything? How could he do that?' I shout at her. 'Answer me.'

She gets a fit of coughing and reaches for the sputum cup. She spits into it. 'It was your father's wish.'

'What?'

'When George asked could he do anything to help in some way, all your father said was the child must never know.'

'He said that?'

Tears are streaming down her face. 'Yes. He was trying to protect you. Your dad, Francis.'

It's Sunday morning. I haven't slept well. I heard Myrtle and Ida laughing at some unearthly hour and then I started thinking about George. I shouldn't be in his house. This place. This guy. All the talk out of him. I'm just biding the moment for him to appear.

I hear a gate opening. I throw off the duvet from Freddy's bed and look out the window. It's not George. It's Myrtle and Ida going down the avenue on their way to church. I know that's where they're going because I look at my watch and it's five to ten.

I wait till the women have disappeared down the avenue and then I open the front door to get the milk. Tomo and John Paul are already outside, sitting on a garden wall.

'Hiya, Franky.'

'Hiya, Franky.'

'Hiya, lads. Up early,' I say.

'We're back from Mass,' says Tomo.

'We got *The Sprinter*,' says John Paul. 'Twenty minutes flat.'

'Freddy stopped going, didn't he,' I say, 'before ...?'

'Yeah,' says Tomo, 'he hadn't gone for ages.'

'Do you know why?' I say.

'I don't think we should really tell you, Franky, not this one.'

'Why not?'

'Well...'

'It's all right, you don't have to tell me.'

'Tell him,' says Tomo.

'Well, it's the same reason why he stopped getting into cars,' says John Paul. 'You remember he ran away from home once? He got fed up of the beatings you know?'

'I know,' I say.

'They got in touch with the priest. I think his old dear told Mrs Dempsey, because he came after him looking for him in his car. He'd gone past the Centre. It was raining and getting dark. All he had with him was the clothes he was in.'

'He was fond of the old dear,' says Tomo.

'He was that, all right,' says John Paul. 'I think he felt sorry leaving her in distress.'

'In distress?' I say.

'At the mercy of his da.'

'Did the priest find him?' I say.

'The priest's car pulls up beside him,' says John Paul. ""Hop in out of the rain out of that," says the priest. *Out of that*, that was a favourite one of his all right. So Freddy hops into the car, glad of a bit of shelter, and the priest drives off away from the avenue to a dark place. When Freddy asks where they are going the priest says somethin' fuckin' mad like, "The world is always going somewhere but we don't always have to follow the world, do we now Frederick?" Do you remember Tomo, he always called him Frederick?

'I do,' says Tomo.

'He says he knew he was mitching, but that he wouldn't report him to the school. He knew all the days and then he gives Freddy a twenty note.

'A twenty?' I say remembering my own offering to him – the same amount, and his hesitation in accepting.

'Yeah. Remember, Tomo, he bought sweets for us after with the money?'

'Yeah,' says Tomo. 'He said they were the dearest sweets he ever bought.'

'"That's for you now," the priest says, "if you do something for me." "What do I have to do?" says Freddy. "I'm going to sing," he says and all you have to do is say, "It's lovely, just keep saying it's lovely." So he starts fuckin' singing in this language. Freddy hadn't a clue what it was and he keeps saying, "lovely, lovely" all the time, thinking of the twenty note. I mean what did Freddy care if he was a nutter, but then he...'

'Then he what?' I say.

John Paul looks at Tomo. Tomo nods.

'Then he puts his hand on Freddy's willy, that's what,' says John Paul. 'Isn't that what Freddy said, Tomo?'

'Yeah.'

'And what did Freddy do then.'

'He thrun himself out of the car. He cut his toe, remember it was all bleedin'.'

'Gushin',' says Tomo.

'And he was soakin' wet, so instead of running away he headed back home. He just followed the light from the Centre.'

'There was no way to go but back,' I say.

'What?'

'Nothing.'

John Paul looks up at me almost with satisfaction. 'Now you know, Franky.'

'Did none of you report him?' I say.

'Report him? What's the point in that? Who'd believe us?'

Cardboard boxes with my things were left outside my house soon after my barring, my navy pair of pyjamas provocatively exposed, and some of my books which were not thrown into a box, were just strewn about on the grass gathering mould. But there were other things like my tooth brush and shaving gear not accounted for. Not crucial stuff, but they all played their part nevertheless in keeping a life intact. And even my lawn mower, come to think of it, why should I leave it for that Ida one to maul?

I can't open the door of my own house. The key won't turn. They've changed the lock. The top bedroom window is open. I fetch George's ladder from his shed. John Paul and Tomo are still on the wall as I go outside.

'Can we give you a hand, Franky?'

'Locked out,' I say as we prop the ladder against the bedroom window ledge. 'Will you bring it back to Freddy's garden when I get up? Will you be able to manage?'

'No problem, Franky.'

The window is a tight fit, but I succeed in sliding through to the clacking sound of aluminium fading below me. I land on the former matrimonial bed and my head hits against something which I perceive to be a dildo. The bed is not made up. There is a pair of bright red pyjamas ensnared in the folds of a mauve nightdress. On the wall, framed, are the words, GROW YOUR OWN DOPE. PLANT A MAN. On the floor are several plastic footballs ripped apart.

I open the back door. I go to the shed which is unbolted and take out my lawn mower and the can of petrol, both of which I lower over the wall into George's garden. Lifting the mower is an effort. It makes my knee give a reminding twinge. I take a minute to draw my breath before returning to the house.

I find a plastic bag in a drawer in the kitchen among other bags folded neatly. I'm afraid to breathe, afraid to disturb anything. The ware in the kitchen is shining, everything in its right place, all harmonising on the oak-veneer dresser.

I wander through the dining room and the sitting-room gathering my bits and pieces. I go up to the bathroom for my shaving gear and tooth brush. The room is transformed: it's like a chemist's shop with its sachets of oils and perfumes and balms and a lady's little turquoise razor cheekily peeping through the aromatic soaps by the bath.

I come down stairs. I'm about to make my way out the front door when I hear a key turning. I push against the vacuum cleaner as I quickly enter the little door under the stairs. Then I hear Myrtle's voice.

'It's only when he started on about foetuses it brought it all back. I mean you know, you know I went up to George. You know all he said to me was, "You can't pin that on me. What about the others you had in the blackberry field?" *They* didn't use johnnies.' "Don't talk to me about johnnies," I said. "Were you too drunk to remember?" And you know what he said then?'

'I know it by heart.'

125

'Jesus, Ida it's all come back to haunt me.'

'Will you stop fretting. We fooled them all, didn't we, although I still think we should've got rid of it. With Dorothy across the water it would've been easy.'

'I know, I know, but ...'

'Look. We did what we did.'

'It's just the way he died. That pylon. And what about Ostrich?'

'You sent the letter?'

'Yes.'

'Remember what I always told you.'

'I know. *Use what you have to get what you want.*'

'So now we have what we want. Close the door, love, there's a draught.'

I quietly tiptoe out of my hiding place and turn the latch on the front door which I leave openbehind me.

It's only now that I'm back in Noreen's kitchen that I notice how rundown it appears compared to Myrtle's. There is a tile missing over the sink, one of those small tiles with the design of chickens on them. The chickens on the tiles don't match. Some are upside down. The vinyl floor is dirty. There are crumbs and a brown stain near the table that looks like a curry mark that was there for a long time. There are dishes unwashed and a chipped mug holding a stale residue of coffee and a cigarette burn on the red Formica top of the kitchen table.

I bring Noreen up her breakfast. Orange juice, tea and toast burnt, as instructed, to a carcinogenic reading of five on the toaster. She is propped up in bed wearing a fresh night dress. She manages a smile as I enter. The sun is shining through the window illuminating the particles of dust in the air and on the carpet.

'I'll hoover the room later,' I say.

'You're spoiling me, Francis.'

'Look, about last night ...'

'It's all right,' she says.

I sit on the chair as she eats her breakfast.

'Did you sleep?' she says

'Not really.'

'I dreamed of you.'

'Yeah?'

'Yes.'

I feel uncomfortable by her forthrightness and her stare.

'It's strange,' I say, trying to steer clear of emotion.

'How do you mean?'

'Our winding up beside you. Myrtle knew?'

'Of course Myrtle knew. She wanted to keep her eye on

127

George.'

'Even though ...'

'Even though he told her where to go. Ida Hourigan weaned her off him eventually. George was disgusted when she moved next door, but what could he do? George couldn't afford to be choosy.'

'You could've sold.'

'It was my mother's house – she insisted on a house instead of the bungalow which was offered to the other cottagers. She was still with us at the time and she didn't want to move anymore. Couldn't blame her really. It's funny, things were okay between George and me when she was alive, well on the surface at least. George respected her. Maybe it was because she swallowed all his lies, but when she died he said to me, *Where to now*? It was like he had no direction. We thought about you. We thought things would be let lie in the past where they belong. That was part of the reason why we didn't socialise much. We thought we could just get on with our lives.'

She pauses, measuring my face. 'She was George's first you know.'

'Who?'

'Myrtle. I was somewhere along the abacus count. Would I have been thirteenth or fourteenth perhaps?'

'I'm sorry,' I say'

'Sorry. Ha.'

'I remember something,' I say, 'in the early days. You must've been in hospital ... I mean the sanatorium. We weren't long moved into the house. I was coming home from work. I had told Myrtle I would be working late, but I got the work done early and I was walking along the avenue when I saw her coming out of your house.'

'Ha,' she says, 'true to form.'

'She looked shocked, the only time I saw her looking like that come to think of it. It was as if I'd caught her off guard. I remember her hair was disentangled and she was pulling at her midriff. "What were you doing in there?" I said. Normally she'd give a quick, cheeky response to any of my questions, but instead she hesitated.'

'She hesitated?'

'Yes. She said she was just tidying up for you.'

'Ha,' says Noreen. 'Welcome to the duped society.'

She coughs into a handkerchief. I see a red stain.

'That's common enough,' she says, noticing my alarm.

'Can I get you anything?'

'I'm okay, thanks.'

'You're sure?'

'Thanks all the same.' She smiles, touches my hand. 'You know the night your mother was killed was the night George proposed. He asked and I said yes just before the accident. It was the last word I said for two weeks.'

'You've no idea where he is?' I say.

She shakes her head. 'Never had.'

'How could he do that, I mean all the years? And you, the way he treats you. I mean I heard sounds.'

'The cries of the damned.' And then, as if suddenly frightened, she adds, 'What I told you, Francis ... I'd appreciate if ...'

'Don't worry,' I say.

There is a smell of stale air in the room, a smell perhaps that only the healthy are conscious of. 'Will I open the window?'

'I'd prefer not. I'm going to run a bath.'

I hold her arms to help her up. 'You are very kind.' Her nightdress is hanging off her frame. I see what purports to be her breasts: empty pouches with little buttons at their ends. She moves her face towards me. I swear she is trying to kiss me. I pretend not to notice her gesture and steady her on her feet.

A shaft of sunlight catches the bedpost, showing up the grottiness of the room. Noreen shuffles in her slippers towards the door. I suddenly realise there is no wallpaper on the walls. They are painted a creamy yellow except for a white space marked by unsmoothed Pollyfilla.

'He must've been doing up the room,' I say.

She turns around, sees me looking at the mark and smiles sort of cynically. 'That's right,' she says 'that's where George was doing up the wall with Freddy's head.'

'Do ... do you know the origin of the blue moon?' Michael says to me in the library.

'That's just a saying.'

'No. It's due to du ... dust particles in the air. When they get big they scatter the light and make a new light which turns the moon blue.'

'So you tell the girls that?'

'Sure. Every time I'd meet one at a dance, I'd say to her, "Do ... do you know what you are?" and she'd say, "No," and I'd say, "You are the once," and she'd say, "The once what?" and she'd smile. They'd all smile, expecting a joke you know like the knock knock who's there jokes, and I'd say, "You're the once in the blue moon."'

Michael's eyes brighten, seeking approval. 'And then I'd tell them how the moon goes blue.'

'And they liked that?'

'Sure. It made them feel special and they'd know tha... that they were appreciated.'

'They knew you weren't being frivolous.'

'Exactly.'

'And they all bought into that?'

He hesitates. 'Well, not always.'

'Not always?'

'At the end of a da ... date ...' he laughs, 'I remember leaving this one to her do ... door. I was hoping she might invite me in but she just turned to me and said, "You're right you know, I am the once, and once is enough."'

Michael treats books with less reverence than I do, but he is more meticulous than I am in cataloguing and putting them in order. Almost obsessively so. 'That's not where you got that,' I

131

heard him saying to a young fellow who was casually dropping a book on a shelf. I discovered later (my curiosity was aroused) that the book in question was actually returned to the correct shelf but was not in its *exact* alphabetical position.

Michael is like me in that he lost a parent at an early age too – in his case, his father, a former civil servant who left himself and his mother with a detached house in the grove. We get on quite well despite the age difference between us and, although I tell him little about my own personal life, he confides in me. He confides especially about his dealings with the opposite sex in which, in his naiveté, he is perhaps most like me, or rather what I used to be.

A year ago he came into the library with his glasses broken (his glasses are so thickly lensed that he is nicknamed *Bottleeyes* by some of the younger and perhaps not so young library members). He told me his current girlfriend (Deborah) had broken them in a rage. He said no more than that. Michael never apportions blame when dealing with girls.

I saw him one night coming from around the back of the avenue. He didn't see me and I never made mention of it.

On another occasion he told me he was in love (with a different girl, a Julianne or some double name like that) only to discover soon afterwards that his 'beloved' was two-timing him. Michael doesn't drink or smoke. He is generous to his girlfriends. He always carries two tickets in his pocket for a music gig or a cinema, usually for Sunday nights, *in case* he has a date and places are booked out, but it was on more than one Monday morning I saw him disconsolately tear the tickets and throw them in the waste basket. His mood swings like a pendulum during relationships. Some Mondays he greets me in a state of euphoria singing *Love me do* which he continues to hum under his breath during library hours and belts out in full throttle when there are no readers present.

But the moments of desolation gradually began to outnumber the moments of euphoria, that is until all of a sudden he met his fiancée, the mystery girl whose name he won't reveal to me.

'Does she live locally?' I say.

'No can tell.' He is teasing me. It's a game, a bit of fun, an attempt to break up some of the tedium of library work. Or maybe he's afraid of naming her (as he did precipitately in his previous relationships), afraid that by so doing she could be scrutinised, and his pain of loss would be all the greater should she let him down as others had done.

'At least tell me what she looks like,' I say.

'You'll see when you come to the engagement party.'

'That'll only be for younger people,' I say.

'There will be older than you there. I wa ... want you there, okay?'

I hear the music as I turn into the grove. I'm carrying a deep-fat fryer in a cardboard box. I bought it quickly in a sale in the Centre. It's awkward but at least it's a practical gift for Michael and his fiancée. The grove doesn't look like a place from which you'd expect loud music to emanate. It has neatly-cut lawns and verges and cherry blossom trees in rows and uniform in height, and houses with their outdoor lights which go on automatically as you pass by them. There is no sign of graffiti or even a spot of dirt in the grove. Just the noise to jar the harmony and to lead me by ear to Michael's house.

When the door is opened, I am blasted by the sound of heavy rock music and I am confronted by Dorothy. She is holding the door handle with one hand and in the other, a glass of something clinking with ice. Her clothes are no longer tightfitting: she's in a wide multi-coloured dress. She looks almost respectable except for the cheap dye which is still in her hair.

'Hello, lurve.'

'I had no idea ...'

She looks at the box. She laughs. 'You always have your hands full, lurve.'

'Is Michael ...?'

'Ah Michael,' she says, 'a thorough gent is Michael.'

A tiny rotund woman in thick-lensed spectacles and carrying a tray of sandwiches appears beside her.

'This is Michael's Mum.'

'You must be Mr Copeland,' the little woman says, raising her squeaky voice through the din.

We shake hands, each of us precariously balancing our loads.

'Michael has told me so...' Her words are drowned out by a

crescendo.

'Pardon?'

'I say he thinks highly of you.'

'I'm happy for him,' I say.

'Pardon?'

'I say it's good to see him settling down at last.'

'Settling down, yes.'

Dorothy turns her head back towards the interior of the house where crowds of young people are milling around the hall. 'Michael,' she shouts in her English voice. In the far corner I could swear it's Ida I see, just the back of her head and her earrings, the rest of her is blocked from view.

Michael appears smiling through a wall of people. His hair is gelled and he is dressed in designer jeans which are too tight and a black T-shirt with *Light my fire* emblazoned on it.

'You met my mam?'

'We met.'

Michael's mam looks proudly at her son. 'If only you knew, Mr Copeland...'

'Francis,' I say.

'If only you knew, Francis, how I prayed.'

'See you later, Mam,' says Michael, dismissively. 'It's ti... time for Francis to meet herself.'

Michael pulls me into the crowd. Some faces turn around and look quizzically at me a I raise the box aloft. He is nodding not quite in tune with the beat which forces him to push his glasses up the bridge of his nose every few seconds. The room is throbbing. I can feel the floorboards lifting. It has a dizzying effect, like being on a swaying ship. So many people thronging, shaking hips, waving arms. Some drunk, tough-looking.

'Here she is,' says Michael.

A blond girl in a navy dress is standing with her back to us talking to other girls. She is swaying slightly – demurely, perhaps one could say – lacking the abandon of many of the other revellers. Michael taps her on the shoulder. She turns around.

'Fra ... Francis, this is Judy.'

I freeze.

'Aren't you going to congratulate us?'

My hand reaches out to touch Judy/Sandra, the fantasy window girl.

Someone calls Michael away. 'Excuse me a moment.'

I glance shyly, almost illicitly at Judy. She looks pale. That's all I can take in as I lower my eyes like a child in shame about to be found out for some misdemeanour. I think of clothes as a great deceiver. I look at the gyrating bones around the room. But I'm uncomfortable standing under her gaze, her confident Ida-like inspection; it's as if my trousers are around my ankles. I feel she knows things.

'I recognise you,' she says.

'What?' I say suddenly alarmed. What has she found out? What am I saying? What is there to find out?

'You're the geezer who asked me for a chip?'

'Yes.'

'You're all right again then?'

'I'm fine,' I say. 'I...'

'I have to thank you,' she says.

'Thank me?'

'Yeah. You made me see him for what he is.'

'See who?'

'The bollocks, who else?'

Michael returns just at the moment of Judy's last utterance. He blushes slightly; he's not used to hearing such language from the lips of a girl. I know him. He tries to hide his embarrassment by talking.

'Show Fra... Francis the ring,' he says.

When Judy raises her left hand I feel faint. It's my mother's ring. I know my mother's ring, the small single cut stone, a modest gem. I remember as a child sitting on her knee fondling the ring, playing with it, twisting it around her finger. And later after her death, to remind me of her, to feel her in the stone, I'd looked at it many times in the jewellery box in my father's bedroom.

'Where did you get this ring?'

Michael looks at me, taken aback my inquisitorial tone. 'A po... policeman wouldn't ask me that.'

'A policeman would,' I say shoving the box into his chest, forcing him to grab hold of it. I push back against the crowd, getting stern looks as I disturb their slow lurch, unentwining arms as tightly wrapped around torsos as the wood of old ivy clinging to tree trunks. Eventually I reach the front door.

'Goin' so soon lurve,' says Dorothy the doorkeeper, still holding a drink in her hand.

Michael doesn't talk to me for days afterwards. He works with a fury (not unlike Myrtle's domestic frenzies). Books are walloped into order on the stacks like bold children and woe betide any poor borrower who leaves a book in the wrong place. It is as if he wants to get the job over with, to hasten the end of every day. I overheard the porter saying that Michael is talking of applying for a transfer to a city library.

I don't know what to say to him. I don't want to jeopardise his chances of happiness, if chances they are. I may be all wrong about Judy. She may be genuine about a new life, but I don't know. I just don't know.

On the third or fourth day of silence (we should receive commendations for following our vocation with such literal fidelity), I say to Michael, 'The ring, I must know where you got it.'

'What is it wi ... with you?' he says, clearly anguished, 'the way you stormed out of my party. You never even said Judy was a smasher or anything. Why are you prying? Look, if you must know, if it makes you any happier, the ring was Judy's grandmother's, Dorothy's mother; you understand it's an heirloom, and Judy wanted it, so I just had to give the money.'

'You paid for the ring?' I say.

'Of course I did. What are you on about? It makes no difference. I wo ... would've had to buy her one anyway.'

'Still no sign of him,' I say as I finish hoovering her bedroom carpet.

'Ne'er a sign or a word. Leave that, Francis.'

I push a button and watch the lead of the vacuum cleaner coil back into its box. 'He must've known you'd tell me. He's afraid to come back.'

'I don't know, Francis. He did his six years.'

'Is that all he got?'

'He'd shrunk and gone all grey when he came out of the slammer. People hardly recognised him.'

'So, even his hair was a pretence. Mr dapper and dandy. And you ...' I say accusingly ... 'you stuck by him?'

'Of course I stuck by him. We had hope then. When you're in prison there's always the hope of coming out, of starting over with a new leaf. Not being recognised suited George down to the ground. The truth of the matter, Francis, was that George Browne was a forgotten person. People forget. There were new kids on the block. New tragedies – aren't there always new tragedies – to concentrate on, one a penny every day.'

'So he thought the past could be buried?'

'Both of us did.'

She sighs. 'And there were other things.'

'What things?'

'His appetites.'

'His appetites, huh.'

'When I got sick, he said I was no good to him, and rows started.' She pauses. 'Then she began calling again.'

'Myrtle?'

'Yes. She'd come along pretending to be neighbourly-like. Even when George told her where to go, she couldn't take a hint. We met you know, Myrtle, George and me.'

'You met. What do you mean, *met*?'

'It was later on after Myrtle had married you. Myrtle told us that she'd led you to believe that the baby had miscarried and that it was yours.'

She waits, gauging my reaction.

'Go on,' I say.

'She told us that you didn't know who the driver of the sports car was, and if no one told you by then, it was unlikely that they ever would. She said you were the easiest person in the world to fool.'

'She said that?'

'Yes. I can say that to you now, but I didn't like to hear her talk like that about her husband. I said it to George afterwards, and he said she was going queer and it was all due to that Ida one.'

Noreen reaches for the 7UP bottle by the bed.

'I'll pour it,' I say

'It's gone flat,' she says. 'It's those plastic bottles. I asked Philomena to get me more. There's a good cut in it when it's fresh.'

'People are beginning to talk,' I say.

'What?'

'Not really talking, more looking than talking. You know when I don't come away like Mrs Dempsey.'

'And what are they saying about the two next door?'

'I don't know.'

She takes my hand and leads it down under the bedcovers. I draw my hand away.

'I'd rather not,' I say.

'Sorry.'

'It's all right.'

She looks pleadingly. 'People stop touching you, you know, when you're ill.'

'Your drink,' I say.

She takes a sip from her glass. 'We entered a pact.'

'A pact?'

'George and I would bring up the baby as our own.'

'You didn't mind, I mean... taking on another person's kid?'

'What was the point in minding? I wasn't able to have children and I really wanted a child, so here was a glorious opportunity. I knew George. By all accounts it was half his anyway.

'But you're not sure?' I say.'

She sighs. 'Can one ever be sure?'

'What is one supposed to believe?' I say angrily. 'Half his, half mine. Which is it?'

'I'm sorry, Francis.'

'I'm talking about Myrtle. Was anything formalised?'

'Nothing. No paper was ever signed. "No way, no way," said George at first, but then Myrtle said she would never broach the subject of the sports car with you, and we agreed to try to live our lives as peacefully as possible. Remember George with his prison record... you know, we had to be careful, although I don't know if George understood the word. Anyway when I consented, Myrtle didn't waste a minute. The baby was landed on us with its umbilical cord still raw.'

'Jesus Christ.'

'I'm upsetting you.'

'Go on,'I say.

'We thought we could eventually afford to move out of the avenue ourselves. But then I got ill. They punctured my lung you know, but it just filled up again. So we went from one year to the next, and the idea of moving out became more and more remote. One year to the next, myself going back and forth to the sanatorium, George going up and down the country, and Freddy growing up on the streets.'

She shakes her head. 'Have you reached there yet, Francis?'

'Reached where?'

'The place of no return?'

'Maybe I have.'

'Poor Freddy. I remember the Halloween party we had the night Melancholy was killed – that unfortunate dog, when I think of what they did to him. It was only afterwards I found out, you know? Only after Freddy's death. Freddy never told me. He never told me things like that, things that happened on the avenue. I think he wanted to protect me from the world, Francis, in his own little way. It was Philomena who told me about the dog.' She coughs. 'It shows us all up.'

'How do you mean?'

'Human beings, Francis.'

She swallows another drop of 7UP and, smacking her lips together, says, 'Anyway, I was going to tell you about the Halloween party.' She looks anxiously at me. 'I'm not detaining you, am I? I mean ...'

'Of course not,' I say

She smiles. 'Well, it was the first time in ages I had been feeling a bit better. I was up and about, so I decided to give Freddy and his friends a little party. I wanted to make a special effort because I'm sure he was tired of seeing me always laid up – not that he ever said anything, ha.'

'It's better than not seeing,' I say. She's struck a chord.

'You mean Myrtle?'

'No, I don't mean Myrtle.'

She looks at me. A little gasp. 'Oh Francis, I'm sorry. I was forgetting.'

There is a sort of apologetic silence for a moment, and then she starts to smile; the smile widens across her face as she remembers. 'I put coins in greaseproof paper and hid them in the curly kale. It was the only time I could get Freddy to eat cabbage. But after a while when they heard the bangers and rockets outside I read that restless look on Freddy's face. What could I do? I could never keep Freddy off the avenue. And they were no sooner gone than some trick or treaters called to the door. George wasn't in, so I answered it, and Melancholy bolted out.'

'I knew that,' I say. 'He ran away from home, didn't he?'

'The dog?'

'No, Freddy.'

'Oh yes. It's well I remember it. George had come home drunk one night spoiling for a fight, and Freddy was just there at the time. George kept calling him a bastard, kept saying that he wasn't his father at all and that he was stuck with him. And Freddy just left. Only for Philomena – she got the priest to find him – only for them we might have lost him even earlier than we did.'

I say nothing. I watch her eyes moisten.

'You know who Freddy's real father was?'

'Who?'

'When all is said and done, who conceived him and reared him?'

'I don't know.'

'The avenue, Francis. The avenue was Freddy's father.'

I put the vacuum cleaner down in Freddy's room and look out on the avenue. Rain is beginning to fall. It comes down as a slow but constant drizzle. John Paul and Tomo are playing a sort of hockey with a small ball and Tomo's brother's crutches. Have they run out of footballs? Have they all been cut up? Tomo's brother sits on the side of the path looking forlorn, not even watching the boys at play. He is looking away into some emptiness of his own, indifferent to the rain dripping from his hair.

Noreen coughs, becomes breathless. I return and hand her glass to her.

'Thank you, Francis,' she says, getting her breath back. 'It's all so easy, isn't it?'

'What?'

'Just to stall for a tiny few moments, imagine without the rise and fall, and it's all over.'

'You're all right now.'

She looks towards the window, silent, perhaps thinking of other worlds not accessible to her. She yawns and her eyes begin to close.

The door bell rings. Mrs Dempsey walks stiffly into the hall carrying her canvas shopping bag. 'I'll leave these in the kitchen,' she says. 'It's just a few things. How is she?'

'Okay,' I say, as she places a new bottle of 7UP and a white sliced pan on the kitchen table.

'I got the sliced 'cause it's easy to toast.'

She hangs her shopping bag on the back of a chair. 'The gardaí are on the avenue,' she says. 'Mr Fitzsimons' house was done last night.'

'That's his name,' I say.

'What?'

'Mr what'shisname. I just remembered that man's name.'

'They did their toilet all over his bed. That's the finish of him, Francis. Mark my words.'

Mrs Dempsey is about to go upstairs.

'She's asleep,' I say. 'I was just tidying the kitchen.'

'I'll do that,' she says, and she takes off her coat to reveal her brown apron tied around her waist. 'There isn't much to wash.'

'How is your hip?'

'The hip is grand. It's only when it gets damp it acts up. Or frosty.' She smiles. 'I can forecast the weather by it.'

'And the new bungalow?'

'Fine,' she says. 'I've just put in the new curtains. You'll have to call.'

'I will,' I say, 'soon.'

'Your dad, Sam, he's not settled at all.'

'I know that,' I say. Every time I'm with Mrs Dempsey she brings up the topic of Dad. I don't want to talk about Dad, not at the moment. I want to talk about me. I want to find out what she knows, what's she's hiding like the rest. I find a dishcloth and proceed to dry the few cups and plates that she washes.

'Did they catch anyone,' I say, 'the gardaí I mean?'

'No,' she says, 'but they're tightening up and not before their time. They're watching the Diamond and the No Ice for selling to minors and for allowing drinking after hours. Do you ever see the cider queues that do be down there on Friday nights?'

'You don't go down there?'

'No, but Father Mack was telling me.'

'When did you see him last?'

'Last week. A call is due. But he was saying the queues do sometimes stretch as far as the avenue.'

She pulls out the stopper of the sink. I hear the belch of the suds as they are expelled through the drain.

'They got rid of the dancing sluts too. You heard about them?'

'I heard something.'

'A downright disgrace, that's what it was, young hussies leading men astray like that, and married men too. Breaking up families, that's what they're doing. Father Mack organised a protest. They picketed the Diamond. I didn't go. I wanted to, but Father Mack wouldn't let me. All the rows down there. God between us and all harm, Francis.'

Mrs Dempsey tries to reach a top shelf with plates.

'I'll do that,' I say.

'Thank you, Francis. That George fella never lifted a hand except when it held a glass of beer. They've been down to the canal a few times,' she says sweeping two thoughts into one.

'Who?'

'The gardaí.'

'They were pelted with stones and driven back. They're afraid to go down there now. It's a frightening thought, isn't it, Francis, to think there are places where there is no law any more.'

As she puts away the last of the cutlery, she says, 'Well, you'll be going home now I suppose. It was good of you to look in on her.'

Is Mrs Dempsey not aware that I have left my own house? Has Noreen not told her?

'I'm staying here, Mrs Dempsey,' I say. 'Don't you know that?'

She looks at me disapprovingly. 'And your father, the poor man? Will you be calling down to him?'

'I'll call down later.'

She shrugs. 'I'll be off so.'

She has her coat half on when I grab her arm and say, 'You knew about him?'

'Who?'

'George. You knew.'

She draws in her breath, her large bosom rising. 'She told you?' she says nodding upwards, 'after all this time?'

'Why didn't *you* tell me?' I say angrily.

'We thought it was for the best.'

'We?'

'Your father and me. You were so young, Francis, and then time ...'

'So how did you meet her?' I say, sensing a slight thaw in the ice barrier between Michael and me.

'Are you going to start re ... recriminating again?' he says.

'No, no recriminations,' I say.

'Swear.'

'I swear.'

He rests the pile of books which he was holding on a trolley and returns to the desk. 'I saw her da ... dancing in the Diamond. I kept going down there and I just watched her. It was cool. But one time I went do ... down and there was someone else dancing instead of her. I asked around. Some fellow called Enda said he saw her going into the dressing room earlier. He made fun of my glasses. He said goggle-eyed bollockses shouldn't be allowed in to see the show, that they had an unfair advantage, or so ... something like that. "Tell her we'll be up later," he shouted, and he gave a dirty laugh. I didn't care. And even though I'd heard about Spikey I didn't fe ... feel any fear. You see I had fa ... fallen in love with her, just from looking at her, you know. It is possible, Francis, isn't it, just by looking at someone to fa ... fall in love? I told Jimmy. You know Jimmy?'

'I know Jimmy.'

'Jimmy is cool. I told him I was her cou ... cousin.' Michael gives a little laugh. 'And, and ... he let me in to see her.'

An elderly woman hands Michael a book to stamp out.

'When I knocked at her door...'

'Sorry, I have another one, love.'

Michael lowers his voice as the lady awkwardly gathers her books into a plastic bag.

'When I knocked at her door she shouted, "Fu ... fuck off."'

146

The lady throws a disapproving look at Michael.

'I heard her crying,' Michael continues, oblivious of the old lady who is moving away. 'I turned the handle of the door and it opened. She was si ... sitting at a table in front of a mirror in a bikini with mascara running down her face. She was trying to dab powder on a cheek which was clearly bruised. "Get the fuck out of here or I'll call Jimmy," she said. "Please," I said. She lifted a steel comb from the dressing table to threaten me. "Jimmy says it's all right," I said. "I ju ... just called to tell you that I admire you, that I lo ... love your dancing, that's all," and I turned to go away. "Wait," she said and her tone had changed, more gentle now, "that's all you wanted?" "Yes," I said. She looked straight into my eyes, and do you know what she said then?'

'What?'

'"Your glasses are cute."'

'She really said that?'

'I swear. And she dried her eyes and ma ... managed a little smile for *me*, Francis you know. "Will you walk me home?" she said. "I'm afraid to go on me own after the last night." She must've thought I was a safe bet with the glasses. "What happened?" I said. "The last night," she said, "was the last straw."'

Michael takes off his glasses and cleans the lenses with a handkerchief. The eyes look strained. 'We avoided the ga ... gawkers in the pub by going out a back door. As we walked along the street she told me what the last straw was. It was after work one night, she was ti ... tired and was coming out of a chipper when her former boyfriend, Spikey, came along and beat the cr ... crap out of some unfortunate fellow who'd asked her for a ch ... chip. She told Spikey to fu ... fuck off, that she was sick of him. "Never again," she said, and then Spikey rounded on her and kept rounding on her every night since because she wo ... wouldn't go back to him. I knew this Spikey was one of the cider-drinkers but I didn't care. Jesus Christ if you saw the cu ... curves on her, Francis, you'd just bow down in adoration.

She could've asked me to walk through fi ... fire and I would've done it.'

A trickle of saliva escapes through Michael's lips and lodges in the hollow of his chin. He wipes it away with the back of his hand.

'There was no sign of the other cider-drinkers as I walked her home. Jesus, she kept her hand on my cr ... crotch all the way as if she was afraid that by removing it I would run off or something. We arrived at her ho ... house, not far from your own, Francis, on the avenue.

'They'd be around the back,' I say.

'Her mother answered the door. You know Dorothy, the English woman? You already met her.'

'I know her,' I say.

'Dorothy said that Spikey was a bastard when she saw the state of Judy's face, and she got ice and called me a thorough gent. She asked me my name. She asked me where I lived. She said I'd have to call again.'

'It was your first time there?' I query, remembering that I'd seen him.

Michael blushes. 'I just went walking up that way once before but I ne ... never went in.'

'Just to look?'

'Ye ... yes.'

'You'd heard things?'

'Yes.'

'Window displays?'

'Su ... sure, but that's all in the pa ... past now.'

Michael banishes his blush, takes a deep breath. 'So that's how I started to call on Judy. After a few dates, Dorothy said she wanted to meet my mother. So herself and Judy called one Sunday evening up to the grove with a cake.'

'What sort of cake?' I say

'*What sort of cake? Where did I ge ... get the ring?* Jesus, what is it, Francis? What are you on? It was an angel cake, okay?'

'Sorry,' I say.

148

His eyes brighten. 'You should've seen Judy in her cl ... clobber. It's just her language that's the problem and it's only now and again it slips. I overheard Dorothy saying to her in the bathroom to watch her p's and q's, that she was dealing with a respectable family now. That was me and my mother she was referring to, imagine. She said it was a chance for her and not to blow it. But it was a ch ... chance for me too, Francis. It's just the people she hung around with, you know, you can't avoid; I mean we use language ourselves; she'll overcome that, won't she, Francis?'

I don't answer.

'Francis.'

'I'm sure she will,' I say.

'Mam was de ... delighted especially after my previous disappointments. They were polite to her. I was pushing on, you know. Mam said she would li ... like to see me settle down, that she was pushing on too. She was afraid she'd die and I wo ... would be left with no one to look after me. You know, Francis, what mothers are like.'

It's Tuesday night. I'm looking out the window of Freddy's room thinking about my father. I had to bring him back to his new bungalow. It was Mrs Dempsey who had alerted me – she found him wandering along the avenue in his slippers. He was looking for something lost way back in his youth, she said, something to do with the War when he worked for a while for relatives of the colonel on an estate in Surrey. It was when in England he first learned the secret of releasing the lachrymal ducts. I read so many times the only letter extant he wrote to my mother (in his microscopic scrawl) that I have memorised part of it: 'They sent me down to London on an errand. I saw devastation all around me. It was the first time as an adult that I shed a tear. I felt ashamed at first, a grown man like me, but when I saw bodies mangled under the rubble of buildings and I heard the orphans cry, I realised, Connie, all the tragedy in the world.'

Mrs Dempsey comes in to dust the room. There's a smell of antiseptic in her wake. I tell her not to bother, that I can do that.

'It's just a lick and a rub,' she says. She gives me a concerned look. 'You're all right?'

'I'm okay.'

'I mean you're not ... angry with me.'

'No,' I say. 'I can deal with it now.'

'Deal with it?'

'Yes, when he comes back I'll ... talk to him.'

'You're not going to do anything silly now, Francis?'

'Now, Mrs Dempsey,' I say, 'when did I ever do anything silly? Wasn't I always the sensible boy?'

'Thank God for that,' she says, and starts to dust around

Freddy's photograph.

I move towards the window. 'I don't see any sign of them,' I say.

'Who?'

'The bingo crowd.'

'There aren't so many going to that anymore. Just oul ones like meself or Mrs Carpenter, and we've stopped going every Tuesday. The hall was half-empty the other night. It's all Women's Studies and Self-Realisation classes now. Self-realisation, I ask you. Aren't some of them leaving it a bit late for that now, Francis?'

I know she is referring to Myrtle, but I say nothing.

Mrs Dempsey finishes her dusting and says, 'I'll be off now. You're not coming?'

'No.'

'Are you not going up to your dad?'

'I got him to bed. He'll be sleeping.'

'I'll look in on him on my way up.'

'There's no need,' I say.

She pauses for a second.

'So you're staying then?'

'Yes.'

She's struggling with her overcoat. Her arm keeps missing a sleeve.

'They'll be talking.'

'Let them,' I say, locating her arm with the sleeve.

'Thank you, Francis,' she says pulling her coat up onto her shoulders. 'Father Mack mentioned you at Mass.'

'By name? I haven't been for a while.'

'No, not by name, but he mentioned about dangers.'

'Dangers?'

'Temptations.'

'Oh yeah.'

'Yes.'

'And did he mention anything about charity?'

'No, not this week.'

A month now and George has not returned. I said it to Noreen a few times. 'Still no sign?' 'No,' she said and I began to wonder as days pushed themselves into weeks and autumn finally ceded to winter, I began to wonder about her words, her wish about his not coming back at all. Maybe he was in a hot clime, on some exotic beach perhaps, chatting up some dolly bird. But he left in anger. Of that I was certain. That was the last thing I remember about George. Perhaps he felt the avenue was closing in on him too. Maybe too many questions were being asked. Maybe the padlock around the avenue's secrets was finally being prised open and George was afraid of what could be found out about him. So, true to form, he scarpered.

Still, I'm waiting. I'm ready for the return of George Browne.

But it is mid winter before we hear about George. Noreen got the news first on her little transistor radio beside her bed. 'George,' she said, staring into oblivion, 'it was on the news.' And she just lay there holding the talking Bakelite, letting it cackle on.

It turned out he hadn't roamed too far after all. He had gone down the country and perhaps he was on his way back home (who knows for certain?), but it wasn't far from the avenue where it all happened.

He was driving very fast in his new car, according to reports. He passed out a motorcyclist. He passed him out by crossing a continuous white line in a congested area. Then he was held up in traffic and roadworks, and the motorcyclist came along and overtook George, in retaliation as it were, and George tried to catch him, and the young fellow was playing games with him, accelerating and then slowing down and swerving to prevent anyone passing him, and George bumped into his shiny chrome and metal. Then the cars all stalled in a line of traffic and the young fellow, his eyes wild, drove up and got off his bike, according to an eyewitness, and came over to George who had his window open, as he always does even on the coldest day (despite his air-conditioning), to let out his cigarette smoke. The guy just went up to the driver's window of George's car and was about to punch or stab or shoot George, we'll never know for sure, because when the guy reached the window, George Browne was already slumped dead over the driving wheel.

Noreen is too weak to attend George's funeral. People call to her to offer their condolences, to tell her how sorry they are to hear about his tragic death so soon in the wake of the other tragedy, how she must suffer and she with her own ill health, her cross is heavy but she will have the reward in the next life. If Noreen had not been sedated, she probably would have said something like, *Look here, there is only the one vile life and this is it,* and she might direct them all to her sink or maybe her sputum cup and give them an audio-visual demo of just how vile this life really is, and if they want to ascertain about another life for her, they are quite welcome to take their spanners and go down on their knees and check the plumbing at the bottom of her drain.

Noreen accepts half-semicosely the touch of hands. There are few kisses. People know; people are afraid. Feeling sorry doesn't mean you have to be foolish.

I meet John Paul and Tomo. They are discussing George. They are speculating on the length of time it will take for George to be devoured in the earth.

'They have to get through the wood first and the brass,' says John Paul.

'That's not real brass,' says Tomo. 'Real brass would cost an arm and a leg.'

'An arm and a leg and a heart,' I say.

'Yeah,' says Tomo.

The same grave as Freddy's. The boys don't like that. They ask me if there is anything I can do.

'Don't let *him* go down in the same place as Freddy,' pleads John Paul and he starts crying.

'They're both dead now,' I say. 'It makes no difference when they're dead.'

Mrs Dempsey and Father Mack see to the funeral. Two gravediggers open the grave by removing the carpet of imitation grass. Freddy's grave, and Father Mack shaking the holy water on it with his aspergillum and murmuring supplications for the faithful to hear. I want to go over to him. The anger is rising in me once more. What is he doing? I want to smash his head with his aspergillum. Freddy's grave. The black marble tombstone with FREDERICK BROWNE, BELOVED SON OF GEORGE AND NOREEN (sic) R.I.P. engraved upon it. Funny that it takes a tombstone to falsify a life. And the space left on the stone to falsify other lives when death decrees.

I'd like to write a little poem for Freddy, something like the ones in those obituary notices, something like. *though all the world you roam, in God's arbour you'll find a home,* something like that, but Freddy did little roaming beyond the avenue. Still, I'd like to express a hope that Freddy would find a place to play, without having to be killed for it, without having electrical currents passed through his body, without being welded to steel.

Father Mack says a few prayers (in just one language). Mrs Dempsey and mourners murmur responses. Myrtle is there, a *safe* distance from me, that is a distance out of reach of *violent* hands. The sergeant is there. What is he doing there holding his cap and looking very solemn altogether? And a little further away stands a sniffling Enda. There are a few stares towards me, a nudge or two from corpulent arms but nothing more. George's death elicits a singular concentration from a huddled mass so no one really appears to be standing apart.

Myrtle is supported (physically) by Ida, who seems to be holding her upright by grasping firmly and pushing upwards her right elbow. Both are dressed in black. It's only the second time for me to see Myrtle in black. The first time of course was when Freddy died. I didn't know then what I know now. Looking now is like reading a book of childhood with adult eyes, and I think of Myrtle not weeping over her child, *her child* (I keep repeating to drill it into my mind), *her child* whom she had abandoned, and I think of her putting all her twisted emotions into the decrying of pylons. And she stands now unsteadily, histrionically almost, as she weeps over a man who abandoned her many years ago.

And she stands like a woman in widow's weeds across from a man whom she won't even reck, a man who is her husband only in name. And I think of her with Ida, and think of time and changing orientations, and I wonder if George had accepted her in the beginning, would Ida Hourigan be holding her so tightly now. Would Ida Hourigan be holding her at all?

As I stand here, I feel like an unwanted shadow, and the years suddenly weigh heavily trying to push me down with George as he is lowered into the grave.

I think I understand what John Paul feared. This big box, this huge adult coffin descending to squash the little box. Freddy was about to receive the final blow from his big daddy landing on top of him.

A wind comes up as I accompany Mrs Dempsey home. The last of the dead leaves on the avenue are tossed in the air like fluttering birds. Mrs Dempsey is unsteady on her feet. A gust nearly knocks her over. I hold her arm, steadying her.

'I should've got a stick long ago,' she says, stooping into the wind, dwindling into a small shape like some protean action enabling her to adapt to nature's severites. 'Too proud,' she says. 'Pride before the fall, what Francis?'

'It's a night for indoors,' I say.

I leave her to her gate.

'It's terrible what they're saying, Francis.'

'What are they saying?'

'About George. They're saying he was killed by his own bastard son.'

'Spikey?'

'Yes.'

'He's George's?'

'That's what they say.'

'But the motorcyclist didn't kill him.'

'I know. That's why they're saying it was him.'

I bring roses to Noreen from Dad's garden. Dad's back in his bungalow after his wandering, but things, as Mrs Dempsey said, are far from right. When I went down to him the other evening, he had his trousers and jacket on over his pyjamas with the cords sticking out.

His roses are small, not at all like the big blooms he used to grow at the cottage. But then what can one expect from unpruned bushes with half dead wood? He came out to the garden with me. He pointed at the roses. There was no torment written on his face this time, just a smile, and he kept smiling when I showed him the black spot on the leaves.

Noreen watches me putting the flowers into a vase.

'Did you ever wonder why they bother to bloom?' she says.

I look at her sighing. I think of Eden and futility and unpolished shoes.

'There's a bird in the sitting-room,' she says.

'A bird?'

'Yes. I could hear it flapping about during the night. It must've been blown down the chimney by last night's wind.'

'I'll go and have a look.'

I go down to the sitting-room, and a small bird – a chaffinch I think – is repeatedly lunging at the window pane, incapable of understanding the invisibility of glass. The bird collapses, almost KO'd on the windowsill. I lift it up. I can feel the warm pulse like a pumping heart. It offers no resistance. I open the window. The evening is growing darker. A light rain has started to fall as I hold the bird outside the window. I try to shoo it away. The bird remains on the outer sill (has it lost the secret of flight?), but after a few moments it flies backwards and lands on the solitary conifer. It stays there, perhaps to summon its strength to face the world, until it becomes invisible in the encroaching rain and darkness.

'Did you get rid of it?' Noreen asks as I return.

'Yes. He was very weak. I hope he made it.'

'Francis of Assisi, that's what you are. Have you no sins? No little blemishes? To make life interesting?'

Suddenly she throws off the bedclothes and lifts her nightdress over her head. Down below her little left pouch I see the bruising on her rib cage. She looks at me with imploring eyes, huge with the madness of illness bulging out of them.

'Lie on me, Francis.'

'Really, Noreen. I mean...'

'What difference does it make now to either of us?'

'I can't, Noreen. I...'

'You'd be doing a good deed,' she says mockingly. 'You like doing good deeds, don't you, my little boy scout. And I am prepared.' She reaches over and produces a condom from her bedside locker. 'There's never a shortage of these around here.'

'I'm sorry, Noreen.' I feel like the bird wanting to escape.

'Not good enough, am I?' She's annoyed now. 'Stuck up, are you?'

'No, Noreen, it's just ...'

Tears form. 'It's years since he ...' She notices me looking at the bruise. 'Except that way of course. What he left me to remember him by.' She stretches her legs out sighing. 'Cobwebs,' she says. 'I just want you to clear away the cobwebs.'

'Come on, Noreen,' I say covering her with the bedclothes. 'We're friends, okay?'

'Friends!' she says. 'Why do you bother?'

I start to tell her about the cider-drinkers, tying to distract her. I tell her about Spikey being near the pylon when Freddy was killed. I tell her what John Paul and Tomo and the other kids felt. She doesn't seem interested. Her mind is lost somewhere.

'Do you ever feel like that, Francis?'

'Like what?' I say.

'Like you're trapped inside a body that doesn't belong to you?'

'Sometimes.'

'Up here,' she points to her head, 'we're all beautiful.'

She pauses, reflecting for a moment, then says, 'I don't blame you... for not wanting to... I mean I wouldn't want me either if I were you, but I'm not you, am I?'

'I guess not.'

'Guess not, ha. I didn't always look like this you know.' She nods to the drawer in the bedside table. 'Take out the photograph.'

I take out a silver-framed photograph of Noreen and George in their younger days, sitting on the bonnet of a red car. Their arms are around each other. She's smiling in a pink summer dress.

'Do you think I was beautiful?'

'A ringer for Audrey Hepburn.'

She smiles.

I examine the photograph again. 'The car,' I say. 'Was it beautiful too?'

Suddenly her smile disappears. 'Oh Francis, I'm so sorry. I don't know what I was thinking of.' She takes the photograph and struggles to return it to the drawer.

'It's all right,' I say. 'I'll put it back.'

I resume talking about Freddy as she just lies there like a corpse. I tell her that we couldn't prove anything, but the kids had asked me to help them. I wasn't quite sure what they wanted me to do, and I had asked George ... 'It's funny ...'

'What's funny?' she says lifting her head, suddenly taking interest.

'He said he would help us when he got back.'

'Typical of the man,' she says weakly. 'He goes off and gets killed when he was needed to do something else. You understand me now, what I said about life. I shouldn't have said perhaps he'll not come back. Maybe I put a jinx on him. We're just little green bottles sitting on a wall, aren't we, Francis? Who'll be next to fall? It won't be me. The long-suffering don't die. That would be too easy. We have to linger on and on.'

'My father's a bit like that.'

'How?'

'He thinks God has amnesia.'

She laughs. 'That's original.'

'When I went down to him the other evening he didn't know whether he was getting up or going to bed, and he said, "God has forgotten me."'

'He said that?'

'It wasn't his first time to say it. He said it before a few years ago in a lucid moment. That's when he got me to fill out the forms for him to join the Tontine society.'

'He's in that?'

'He kept pestering me. He said, "If God has forgotten me I may as well make capital out of it."'

'He's not too badly off.'

'How do you mean?'

'He believes there's someone there.'

I walk to the window to stretch my legs. The curtains are drawn in the houses opposite.

'You never draw your curtains,' I say. I look across at her bed. It is positioned so she can have a view out.

'I may as well lie in a tomb if I can't see the day or the night, for what they're worth. You know what the day is, Francis?'

'Wednesday.'

'Wrong,' she says. 'The day is the cloud every day and the night is the torment.'

'George kept saying you can't prove anything,' I say, trying to avoid falling into her slough of despond. 'George said he went to the gardaí but he never did.'

'You know why?'

'He had a prison record.'

She smiles wryly.

'I have some idea,' I say.

'Ah. What is your idea?'

'Judy,' I say

'Judy?'

'The one across.'

'You mean the exhibitionist, the one who torments me from her window?'

'Torments?' I say, turning around.

'She knows I am an invalid, that I can do nothing. She holds the men of the avenue by the balls. Many's the night he left us short over that one.'

She pauses and looks directly into my face. 'You don't mind my saying *by the balls*, do you?'

'No,' I say, but I feel my face reddening slightly by her direct look.

'And tell me, Francis, did you not fall under her spell too, or was it that you never noticed?'

The handle on the bedroom door is hanging off. 'Is there a screwdriver?' I say, avoiding her question.

'What?'

'That door handle.'

She gives a little laugh. 'Ha. George had tools in the shed for all his loose screws.'

The shed is open. Its black door peeling paint. I find the screwdriver. I look at my mower, a guest in a new habitat, just like me. I look for its sustenance, its can of petrol, but there is no sign of it.

'George and his fast cars,' she says as I tighten the screws on the door handle.

'The shed...' I say. I'm about to ask is it normally locked but she is half delirious, almost asleep. Sweat is pouring down her face.

'The punishment is the world.'

I dampen a towel in the bathroom and dab her forehead. I wonder should I call a doctor but she is sleeping now, snoring gently. I want to go home, to my own place. I want to escape the hospital that is her house: the stale air, the smell of illness that never improves. I want to flee from her pessimism, her growing sarcasm, from the repulsion of touching old bones.

I t's bin day when the inevitable happens. Myrtle and Ida are coming out the front door of forty eight as I'm putting out Noreen's half-full (half-empty?) dust bin. They walk by cocking their noses.

'Look where the Ostrich is buried now?' says Ida out loud, holding firmly onto Myrtle's arm.

'That letter ...' I say.

Myrtle, still dressed in black, glances at me as I stand motionless, my hands on the bin; but she keeps walking, saying nothing.

Ida's voice tails off. 'Even his oul fella has kicked him out.'

They're going to get their hair done I bet, or rather to get Myrtle's hair done. Ida always does Myrtle's hair. She has her own hairdressing salon in the Centre. She calls the shop *Céline's*. Myrtle said (in her talking-to-me days) that a customer asked for Céline once to do her hair and Ida said she wasn't in that day and they had a titter at the woman's expense. So ever since then, anytime there is something recriminatory or something they don't want to be involved in, they say, 'That must have been Céline,' or 'Céline did that'.

Ida called her salon *Céline's* to sound posh. Besides, Ida was never happy in the way she got her name. Myrtle says it was her father – a drunken lout – who insisted on calling his daughter after some old flame he knew before he was married, and when he got drunk he would whine like a dog after her – the old flame that is – and call out her name, and that was even with her mother, his wife present. He didn't care. The alcohol unhinged him.

The bin is empty when I come home from work. I'm wheeling it in when I see Tomo and John Paul sitting on the

162

garden wall.

'Hiya, Franky.'

'Hiya, Franky.'

They know I'm staying with Noreen. They know but say nothing, out of respect, I would like to think.

They have a pent-up look about them. They are bursting to tell me something.

'Do you know what we saw?' says Tomo.

'No,' I say.

'We saw Ida Hourigan kiss a girl.'

'Where?'

'In the hairdresser's,' says John Paul.

'We're passing by the window,' says Tomo, 'and there's this girl...'

'Sue Ellen's older sister,' adds John Paul.

'Sitting on a chair, and Ida's cuttin' her hair...'

'And she puts the scissors and comb down,' says John Paul, 'and then she comes up to her and puts her two hands on her shoulders and gives her an almighty smacker.'

They both laugh.

'Yeah. On the lips,' says Tomo.

'And what does the girl do?' I say.

'She jumps up and wipes her hand across her mouth and runs home,' says Tomo.

'With her hair half-cut,' says John Paul.

'And her old dear comes down afterwards with her rag out,' says Tomo. 'We all followed down.'

'But you know what Ida says?' says John Paul.

'What?'

'"You must be talking about Céline. She's not here," she says, cool as a cucumber.'

'Cool as a cucumber?'

'That's what the old dear said. "It *was* you," she says, and you know what Ida does?'

'What?'

'She laughs in her face, Franky. "Prove it," she says. "It's just

163

your word against mine.'"

'Was no one else there?' I say.

'No one.'

'And the woman went away,' says Tomo.

I look out the window of Freddy's room. Darkness is falling. A helmeted motorcyclist with his visor down is coasting up the avenue, checking houses. He slows down outside number forty eight, dips into his pannier with his left hand and, like a paperboy doing his round, throws a football into the garden. He beeps once, turns the bike around and, revving smoothly, without the engine snarl typical of most bikers, disappears into the darkness. The kids – the few remaining out at this hour – are down the far end of the avenue. They are too engrossed in a game, or else it is too dark for them, to notice the motorcyclist.

The door of forty eight opens and Ida steals out, looking left and right before picking up the ball. Gauging its weight in her hands, she slips back like a phantom into the house.

It's Tuesday night, twenty to eight, and Ida and Myrtle are walking down the avenue. Myrtle is wearing one of her old coats and a scarf and carrying a shoulder bag. Ida as usual is in her denim jeans and jacket. Dorothy joins them at the end of the avenue.

I check on Noreen. She is sleeping with *The Age of Reason* open with its pages splayed like an accordion between her fingers. Her breathing is heavy coming through her open mouth.

I remove the book, tuck Noreen in, go downstairs and close the front door gently after me. I follow the women down the avenue. Stepping in and out of shadows, I close the gap between them and me to about a hundred yards. Sue Ellen accosts me on the avenue. It's the wrong time, Sue Ellen, but I can't say that to her. She never calls me by my name, not like the other kids; she never gives me any title; it's as if it's all understood, part of an unwritten agenda.

Sue Ellen is changing Sandra's clothes.

'Hello, Sue Ellen.'

'Mammy and Daddy had a row.'

'What about?'

'About my sister, and Sandra did a pee pee in her pants.'

I say goodbye to Sue Ellen and quicken my pace until I catch sight of Myrtle and Ida once more. They pass Saint Anthony's Hall without as much as a glance in its direction. I follow, keeping a safe distance. They pass the school near the Centre where voices emanate from classes. They don't even pause to listen.

They are walking fast. With a purpose you might say. This is different to the sauntering way they walk to church or to the hairdressers. There is no linking this time. I wonder if perhaps there is a coolness between Myrtle and Ida as a result of the salon kiss which Myrtle may have found out about. Difficult to gauge a mood by one's gait.

They are heading towards the canal.

They have crossed the bridge and are going towards the cider-drinkers. There is a fire burning by the canal and several cider-drinkers are sitting around, taking deep slugs from flagons. Spikey is there. The women approach him.

I stand concealed behind some briars on the other side of the water and watch the women talking to Spikey and to another cider-drinker. Spikey takes a wad of notes out of his leather jacket and hands the notes to Ida. Ida counts the money. The other cider-drinker is holding a flagon. Ida nods to Myrtle and lodges the money in a pocket of her jacket. Myrtle then opens her shoulder bag and takes out a packet which she hands over to Spikey.

I move away, but as I'm turning someone shouts, 'There's some fucker over there.' I walk fast, mustn't run, that would draw more attention to myself. Besides, I know the distance between them and me is too great for them (even running) to overtake me.

Stones are thrown in my direction, but they plop tamely in the water.

A few more shouts.

'We'll get ya.'

'Ya fuckin' spy.'

Things are quiet in the library today. Just a few elderly women dropping in to replenish their dose of romances on their way to or from their shopping, and a couple of unemployed men who call in for a free read of the newspapers. I'm thinking of Myrtle: my wife, the drug pusher. I'm thinking of what to do. How to word it for the ruddy-complexioned sergeant. *And what makes you think, Mr Copeland, that your wife is dealing in drugs?*

Michael is humming *Love me do* at the stampout desk and flicking through a book. That heavy rock stuff at the party wasn't Michael. He's too much of an innocent, too much of a square for that sort of thing. I'll have to talk to him, warn him about what he's getting himself into. But how to do it without his taking umbrage?

'What's the book?' I say.

'*The Kama Sutra*,' he says.

'You didn't get that here.'

'Ju... Judy gave it to me.' Michael's eyes twinkle. 'She's terrific, Francis. She's so ... uninhibited.'

'She would be, wouldn't she?'

Michael tuts. 'I told you she's fi... finished with that business. She works in *Céline's* now with her mother and her aunt Ida.'

'Did you set any date?'

'Date?'

'To get married?'

Michael closes his book.

'We've already ti... tied the knot, Francis.'

'What?'

'Last Friday. Judy told me not to te... tell anyone yet. I was going to tell you after a while.'

166

'Wait now,' I say, 'you're telling me you're married?'

'What was the point in waiting around, that's what Judy said, and she doesn't mind moving into the grove even with Mam there. Judy's good like that you know; she's not a fusspot, Francis. And there's plenty of room.'

'No ceremony?'

'Judy didn't want any commotion... you know after the...'

'What's the point...?'

'What?'

'... in hanging around?' I say *hanging around* quickly. I don't know why I say that, it's just to fill a gap. I don't mean it that way. But I'm afraid to leave things raw, afraid of hurting him.

'It's just Judy, you know, she wanted to make it legal. Anyway we already had a ba ... bash.'

'A bash?'

'Fo ... for the engagement I mean. Why go to unnecessary expense? That's what Judy says. So it was ju ... just nice and quiet with Mam there and ...'

'She didn't mind?'

'Well she would've preferred a church wedding, you know Mam, but it was okay. She said everyone has a right to his or her beliefs.'

'Or the absence thereof.'

'She was ju... just happy for me, you know. I don't mind telling you, Francis, it was a relief to all of us. I thought I would lose her like... well you know, and Ju... Judy kept saying that Spikey could come along at any minute to break us up, but he can't do anything now that it's all legal. Isn't that right, Francis?'

A book appears on the returns desk. I open it at the due-date page and find myself staring at a buff envelope. It bears no stamp, just the words, THE LIBERARY MAN misspelled in capitals. I look up. There is no one there. Inside the envelope is a torn sheet of white, lined paper with writing, again in capitals

RAT AND YOU ARE BROWN BREAD
REMEMBER THE BOWLER
REMEMBER FRED

I feel a little shiver running through me but nothing more than that. They are just words, just ink on a page. A rhyming joker.

Michael looks at me standing abstractedly, still holding the envelope.

'You ... you all right?'

'I have to go out,' I say. 'You'll be able to manage?'

'No problem.'

'Did you see anyone?'

'Li ... like who?'

'Anyone suspicious I mean, around?'

'No.'

'If my father calls ... just write down for him that I won't be long.'

The sergeant is sitting behind the desk in the garda station as I enter. I firstly ask him if he has any information on the theft from my father's house. 'Not yet. Working on it.'

The phone rings. 'Hang on till I get this down,' he says unscrewing the top of his fountain pen. 'What time was she spotted?'

I resist the temptation to sit on the solitary chair as the sergeant talks. Chewing gum speckles the floor and there's a stale smell pervading the room. When the sergeant puts the phone down I show him the letter. I explain the reference to the dog and to Freddy. He asks me have I any idea what prompted such a letter, so I tell him about what I saw at the canal and how I was seen.

'By gee,' he says, 'it's all happening down there.'

Slowly, he writes the details in the book. I have this feeling that at any moment he's going to ask me to spell something. His huge hands seem to be suffocating the pen, squeezing its last drops of life-ink onto a page.

'Two women,' he says. 'And one of them your wife?'

'Yes.'

He looks up at me, raises his eyebrows.

'We're separated.'

'And the cider-drinkers gave them money?'

'Yes.'

'And they gave a packet in return.'

'Yes.'

'And you think it was drugs?'

'Yes.'

'Why, Mr Copeland, do you think the packet may have contained drugs?'

169

'Because of the football. Remember I reported to you before?'

'Oh yes. Now I remember your coming in. What date was that?'

'I don't know.'

The sergeant looks at me as if I have two heads.

'I can't remember.'

I feel the weight on my chest again. Why doesn't *he* know? That's his job. I feel a futility in things, in words, in communication.

He flicks through the pages of the book.

'Ah yes, the report is here.'

The sergeant smiles and screws his fountain pen back into its top.

'Don't worry,' he says, 'everything is ...'

'Under investigation, I know.'

The sergeant suddenly looks peeved. 'Do you know, Mr Copeland?'

'What?'

'You say you know. Do you know that files must be put together on all these reports. Statements must be taken – not just from you – and anything found is catalogued for forensic analysis. You're a librarian, aren't you? How much time does it take for you to catalogue your books?'

'Quite a while.'

'Good day, Mr Copeland,' he says victoriously.

As I come out of the garda station, I see Spikey sitting on his motorbike watching from across the road. He's not grinning this time, nor is there any sign of a blade. When he sees me, he revs hard and speeds away.

I head back towards the library. The world is running on autopilot, or maybe it's just my life. I feel I'm losing whatever little handle I have on things. I'll have to talk to Michael. Also I'll have to get advice about Myrtle and about the house.

It's time to shake off sand.

Mrs Dempsey comes along, carrying her shopping bag, heading for Noreen's. I don't want to delay.

'Did you hear the latest?' she says.

'The latest?'

'Your library assistant and that Judy one...'

'I've heard. Look, Mrs Dempsey, I'm in a bit of a hurry.'

'We were coming home from bingo last Tuesday evening, Mrs Carpenter and myself, and we met them,' she says, paying no heed to my words, carried away as she is now on a gossip wave. 'We stopped to admire the engagement ring, but do you know what?'

'What?' I say huffily. I feel anxious. I want to get back to work.

'It was *two* rings she showed me. Could you credit that now, Francis?'

I smelled the smoke before I saw the flames. Heard the bell of the fire brigade passing. Heard the impatient hooting of car horns and then the piercing *weehoo weehoo* of an ambulance. Heard shouts, even a few screams. I saw John Paul and Tomo and some of the avenue kids running.

I saw films before of great fires. Infernos where the powerful heat of the flames makes the air tremble visibly and gives a surreal quality to everything surrounding it. That's the way I see the library now. I can't believe it's for real. People and buildings are covered by a haze, a shimmering veil which renders things untouchable, which makes one think that what is happening is a sort of chimera, and that soon the veil will lift when the soaring heat has abated and things will once again be as they were before.

Michael runs towards me, his hair and face blackened like a coalman's.

'Your fa ... father, Francis ...'

'What?'

'He was caught by a falling beam.'

'What are you saying?'

'I tried to lift it off him but it was too heavy.'

Michael gets a fit of coughing. He holds a handkerchief to his mouth. 'I'm so ... sorry, Francis.'

Through the smoke and vibrating film of air I see a stretcher being carried past firemen with hoses thrusting against the enveloping flames.

'Dad,' I shout.

'Stand back please,' says a stretcher bearer.

In the ambulance drips and tubes are hanging out of my father as he breathes through a mask. His cap has gone, his silvery hair hanging in streaks.

'How did it happen?' I say to Michael who is crammed contritely beside me.

'Spi ... Spikey soaked the books in petrol.'

'Spikey.'

'I'm so ... sorry, Francis.'

'Don't keep saying that.'

His glasses are hanging off his nose with one of the arms missing.

'It all happened so fast. Things were quiet. I was just reading, then suddenly out of the blue I saw Spikey coming with a can of petrol. He started to shake the can over the books. I ra ... ran over and he knocked me down.' Michael rakes his hair with his fingers. 'I couldn't do anything. He ju ... just struck a match off the zip of his jacket and threw it and ran, and your fa ... father ...'

'He was in the library then?'

'He had come up the stairs a little while before the fire broke out. He was anxious to tell you something. He was all excited. He sa ... said he was the last. "The last what?" I said, but he of course couldn't hear me, so I wrote down that you'd be back in a little while, like you told me, and he was waiting around.'

Impervious to the smells, I sit by my father's bedside in the intensive care unit of Blanchard town hospital. The room is darkened with just a little red light on a wall. I'm trying not to think of smells. I think of breaths. I count the breaths, the little pulse ball bleeping on the monitor. Life. I hold my father's hand. His face under the oxygen mask looks so old now, so truly vulnerable. A nurse comes in soundlessly, checks his chart, smiles at me. There is calm in the night. Peace with a touch of hope in the sound of the bleep.

His notebook is lying with a few of his possessions on a little table by the bed, scarred charcoal, corners burned, a fault on the line in the communication link to an old, deaf man. *Did you lock the front door after you?* What did I really want to say? What is it, Dad? What is it in your head? Is it some chemical in our makeup that makes some people sad and other people glad? What did I want to say to you all the years? I'm sorry, Dad, for letting Myrtle treat you the way she did. It was wrong. I wanted you to be strong, Dad, so that I could be strong. You are strong, Dad. You came through fire.

W e sit on high stools in the Diamond. The place is quiet, only a few people in the pub, maybe due to the absence of the dancers.

I sip my Bushmills, holding the liquid for a while on my tongue as if I'm trying to recapture something, freezeframe lost moments, trying to banish a growing sense of desolation.

Michael takes a gulp from his glass and coughs.

'It takes a bit of getting used to,' I say.

'It was all because of me,' he says. 'I drew that fellow on us.'

'Things happen,' I say and I down my whiskey.

'Let me get you another one.'

'There is one thing I remember,' I say rather emotionally, 'when I was very small, maybe four or five or maybe six or seven ... oh I don't know.'

'It doesn't matter, Francis.'

'It does matter,' I say, surprising myself by my own abruptness. 'I used to follow him about as he worked in the garden. I had built up a store of plant names which I had learned from him, and I used to throw out the names to impress him you know.'

'You were a little show-off,' says Michael teasingly.

'Maybe I was. Maybe like you with your facts.'

Michael smiles. 'Maybe.'

'Anyway, I remember this smell, this wonderful scent. It's funny how it's the smells we remember, Michael, isn't it? Anyway this wonderful scent was coming from a tree in the summer garden. "It's lilac, Dad," I said. "No, no," my father said very seriously, "that's not lilac, it looks like lilac but it's not lilac; it's the wrong season for lilac. That's buddleia," and a butterfly landed on the tree. "And that's the Meadow Brown," he said.

175

Jesus, Michael when you think ... he knew the names of everything.'

Michael catches Jimmy's eye. 'The same again please.'

'How will the new kids know things, Michael?' I say.

'How do you mean?'

'The fields are buried and the trees are chopped down.'

'I don't know, Francis?'

'Freddy knew things,' I say.

'Who?'

'A kid on the avenue.'

'Oh, the kid who ...?'

'Yes. He knew things like that.'

Jimmy arrives with the drinks. 'Sorry to hear about your father. I hope he'll be all right?'

'Thanks.' I say.

'A great old timer. A great patron, but listen,' he says, lowering his voice, 'I don't want any more ... rumpus. *Capisce*? Cost me a few bucks.'

'It won't happen again.' I say. I had almost forgotten about the circumstances of my last visit to the Diamond.

'Guys are barred for less,' Jimmy says, 'but seeing you have your own troubles ... I never hit a man when he's down. This one's on the house. To your old man.'

'That's decent of you.'

'Thanks very much,' says Michael, delighting at the unexpected generosity.

Jimmy moves away.

'What rumpus?' says Michael.

'A little fracas, ' I say, 'forget it.'

Michael smiles. 'You're deep, Francis.'

Jimmy comes back wiping a cloth along the counter. 'How is your cousin?' he says to Michael.

'My cou ... cousin?'

'Yeah.'

'Oh, she's fi... fine.'

'The show's closed down,' he says. '*Kaput*. Bloody protesters, led by the parish priest. Carried placards they did outside the pub. It wasn't worth that. Sure you can get stronger stuff than that on videos now. There was no harm in it.'

The word sounds like *harem*, the way Jimmy pronounces it as two syllabled.

'It's what went on after hours and on the streets, they should've placarded. Picking on innocent people trying to make a few bucks I mean...You have to turn a blind eye sometimes. They say she got married.'

'Tha ... that's right,' says Michael.

'No disrespect to you being her cousin and all but I pity the guy who got her.'

'Wha ... what do you mean?' says Michael

The barman winks. 'She was controlled. *Capisce?*'

Michael opens his mouth and is about to say something. It is clear by the hurt look on his face that he is about to challenge Jimmy, but Jimmy is called by a customer at the far end of the bar.

'He didn't have to ta ... talk like that, to say those things. They're not true.'

'They *are* true Michael,' I say. 'That's why I have to ask you one more time about the ring.'

Michael tuts loudly. 'Not again. You said no more recriminations, remember?'

'It was my mother's.'

'What?'

'The ring. It was stolen.'

'No way.'

'Afraid so, Michael.'

Michael slams his glass on the counter. 'That's not true. You'd better be ca ... careful with your accusations. Look, I'm so ... sorry about your father, but I have to go.'

Dad's okay. The beam didn't puncture anything; he's just suffering from too much smoke inhalation. He's in a ward now, temporarily of course, propped up with an amount of pillows. He even manages a smile for me when I visit, just a hint. Could the jolt have released something? I have a new notebook for him. I write on the very first page: HOW ARE YOU DAD? He looks at the words, nods. He understands.

I'm staring out Freddy's window, still thinking of the fire. I'm wondering what the gardaí are doing? Are they acting on any leads? Or is everything *under* investigation? Swept under. Speaking of which, a garda and bangarda have appeared and are walking down the avenue. The sun is shining. It's unnaturally warm for this time of year. The garda, a young fellow, is not very tall, like a lot of recent recruits. He is joking and laughing with the bangarda (also young) as they walk along. Except for the uniforms they would almost pass for an item. The kids are playing with a soft mucky ball. They must have run out of good footballs or else they have been cut or impounded.

The ball goes high in the air. The garda takes off his cap and hands it to his laughing companion and pursues the ball, keeping his eye on it all the time until he skilfully catches it, hugging it close into his chest

I can see by the sulky look on the faces of the boys that they are not impressed. They don't handle a ball, except for their goalie. A ball is meant to be moved by foot. They don't like the fuzz on their avenue. They like it even less when the fuzz pretends not to be fuzz. They don't like anyone taking their ball. They stand sullenly until the garda's smile abates. He's had his fun, so they are waiting for him to hand their ball back and don the mantle of garda again.

But the garda, holding the ball in the crook of his left arm, suddenly plunges a penknife through it.

The kids shout, protesting, and the bangarda says something to them, but there is nothing inside the ball, and the garda hands them back a ruptured globe with an apology and a coin.

I'm on the bus heading into a city library. It's a provisional arrangement for Michael and me until our own library is repaired, however long that may take (if ever), depending on funds, depending on priorities; the smaller suburban library of course loses out to the bigger, multi-purpose city libraries.

The same woman with the brolly is on the bus queue.

'Hello love,' she says, 'are you still wondering?'

Michael is in the library before me, stacking shelves. He doesn't greet me.

'Tell me about plastics,' I say to him, brushing aside the memory of our previous altercation. 'You're good on facts.'

'Plastics?'

'Yeah.'

'How do you mean plastics?'

'How things are made like, how they are moulded.'

'You mean like buckets and basins and things?'

'Yeah.'

'And plastic hips and plastic cider flagons.'

'Yeah, and footballs.'

'Footballs?'

'Yeah. How are footballs made?'

'You know what molecules are?'

'No,' I say.

'Molecules, Francis, they're made from molecules. Why don't we go down to the factory after work.'

'I thought all those things were imported,' I say

'No. Biggs & O'Connor.'

'I've seen the name but I never realised ...'

'I'll show you. It's just beyond the Centre,' he says. 'How's your Dad?'

'He's on the mend,' I say.

'Good,' he says, cheering up, feeling a confidence in his new role.

We walk to Biggs & O'Connor, a half mile or so from the Centre on the busy main bus route to the city. It's a sprawling place half occluded by high railings and conifers. A middle-aged fellow with a white coat welcomes us at reception.

'We're only here to see the process,' I say, 'if you don't mind.'

'No problem, no problem at all, sir.' He winks. Does he think we're sales people or something?

'In here,' he says. We go into a room where we are given white coats and hats. 'Standard procedure,' he says. I feel like one of those clinical psychiatrists about to enter an asylum ward to give a lobotomy to some unfortunate patient. We go out to the factory floor and I'm immediately attracted by the smell of molten plastic. I could come here every day for a quick fix. A young fellow is taking sheets of plastic from heating rollers that look like hardened water in a waterfall under the fluorescent light.

'You see?' Michael says, pointing to a blue lava. Michael is shouting, trying to make his voice heard through the noise of machines. 'That's the molten pool,' he says. 'That's where your footballs come from.'

There are several women and a couple of men also in white uniforms and hats working at conveyor belts, checking as the plastic comes out from the mould. Checking for what?

'It's when the plastic is added the pigment is added,' Michael says.

'The pigment?' I say.

'Yeah, you know the black and white footballs.'

Michael is talking to the official who welcomed us in. He is showing great interest in what the official is saying. He looks so untypically self-assured. There is no stammer as he speaks. 'Time, temperature and flow,' the official says, and Michael nods, understanding.

I think of the terms: *lava* and *pool* and *time, temperature* and *flow,* and wonder are we really talking about a plastic world?

'It's called extrusion,' Michael says to me.

'What?'

'The way it's done. The way the plastic is...'

'I know,' I lie.

I look at the people on the conveyor belt. One woman places something into an unsealed football as it passes along. I look closely at the woman. I swear it's Dorothy. She catches my eye and lowers her head under her hat. She starts fidgeting with her fingers in between jobs. I follow the course of *her* football along the belt to its final sealing and watch as it is machine-lifted and stacked secure among all the new-born gladdeners of childhood innocence.

'Do you know who's over there?' I say to Michael.

'My mother-in-law of course.'

'You never told me she worked here.'

'I didn't think you'd be interested,' he says, 'judging by the way you go on about Judy.'

He waves over to her and she (slowly as if reluctant to reveal herself) waves back.

I go down to the garda station. I report about the plastics' factory. I tell the sergeant what my suppositions are and I tell him I saw Dorothy. 'Dorothy?' says the sergeant. 'What was her surname?' 'I think it's Murphy,' I say remembering a reference to her by Mrs Dempsey. 'An interesting family,' he says looking across at me with a touch of a sneer.

I tell him I saw Dorothy placing something in a football before it was sealed.

'So, you're saying these plastic footballs are transporting heroin?'

'Yes.'

The sergeant ponders, touching his lips with his pen. 'Can you be sure?'

'Sure? No, I can't be sure.' There he goes again. 'But it was a small packet of something and it warrants an investigation into the matter, an immediate investigation.'

The sergeant gives me a look from under his eyes. 'Immediate, you say?'

'Yes.'

'And tell me this, Mr Copeland, how are we to distinguish these footballs from all the hundreds of thousands of others that are produced?'

'Examine the seams,' I say

'The seams?'

'The ones with the heroin have seams.'

And then I tell him about the courier on the motorbike coming up the avenue and stopping at Mountain View.

'Mountain View?' says the sergeant.

'The name on my house, number forty eight. Well, the house where I was living before...'

183

'Where your wife is living now with her... eh... friend?'

'Yes.'

The sergeant looks at what he's written. 'So this motorcyclist stops outside what was your house?'

'It still is my house.'

He gives me that peeved look again. 'Can you give a description of the motorcyclist?'

'No, it was too dark. Just... the leather gear.'

'Where were you viewing from?'

'The Brownes' house next door.'

'The house next door?'

'Yes. The top bedroom window.'

'And why were you there?'

I feel my pique rising. 'Can't we just stick to the...?'

'I beg your pardon.'

'I'm staying there,' I say.

'With the widow Browne?'

'What are you implying?'

'I'm implying nothing, Mr Copeland. Now could you explain briefly and calmly ...'

I tell him how I wound up in Noreen's. He's taking delight in this. Stopping me for clarification every few words simply to embarrass me. I should have just told him I was having it off with Noreen. It would have made everything simpler.

'What did the courier do when he stopped his motorcycle?'

'He took a football out of the side pannier and threw it into the garden.'

'Of Mountain View?'

'Yes,' I say, sensing the desperation in my voice.

'Just the one football.'

'I'm not sure. There were two panniers, one on either side of his bike, so maybe in the dark he could have thrown more, but I only saw the one.'

I tell the sergeant about Ida coming out and looking up and down the avenue before picking up the ball ('Just one ball?' 'Yes, I've already said...') and how, before bringing it into the house, she examined it.

'For seams?' he says.

'Yes.'

I tell the sergeant about all the footballs that have been punctured and ripped apart in the master bedroom of Mountain View, *my* bedroom I emphasise, and I'm nearly going to add about the dildo but I refrain. I tell him about the duo's walk to bingo which was not a walk to bingo, and he stops me again for clarification, and I get more frustrated because he blocks the flow of things, and I tell him that the walk to bingo is really a walk to the canal which leads to the transfer of goods – that is drugs for cash – with the king of the cider-drinkers.

'The king of the cider-drinkers?'

'Spikey,' I say, and for the first time saying his name it feels inadequate. I mean could that name hold up in a court of law?

'And his real name?' the sergeant says, as if reading my thoughts and writing away.

'I don't know,' I say.

He stops writing and looks up and smiles.

'It's Philip Hanratty,' he says.

'You know?'

'Yes.'

'And what are you asking me for then?'

'To gauge how much you really know, Mr Copeland.'

The sergeant taps his pen on his lips. 'Philip Hanratty. We know that gentleman all right.'

Suddenly Spikey is no longer Spikey; he is someone else; someone humanised, with a Christian name and a surname.

'And now, Mr Copeland is there anything else you wish to say?'

'Can you tell me about Freddy Browne?' I don't know why I say that. Maybe it's because if he knows about Philip Hanratty he may also know about Freddy.

'What do you want to know?' he says

The sergeant gives me a look, the superior look of somebody who has one up on you.

'I...' Suddenly I've lost my nerve. I can't ask the question because I'm afraid of the answer.

'Well, Mr Copeland?'

'He was George Browne's son, wasn't he?' I say.

'Yes,' he says, and pauses before adding, 'in name.'

'In name?' I say. 'What do you mean by that?'

'As I say, there *are* some things we do know, Mr Copeland.'

'But...'

'It wasn't for us to interfere in domestic matters, you understand? Such a tragic death. May he rest in peace now.'

'But... how long have you known this?' I say.

'You should talk to your wife.'

'How can I talk to my wife?' I exclaim angrily. 'There's a bloody barring order against me.'

'I'm sorry, Mr Copeland. I can't help you there.'

'**A**re you all right, Francis?' she says. 'Even I look better than you.'

'You knew,' I shout at her. 'You knew all along.'

'Knew what?' she says, alarmed at my tone, trying to prop herself up in the bed.

'Don't give me all that innocent stuff,' I say. 'You knew who Freddy's father was. You bloody well knew it was me.'

'You?' she says. 'Where did you hear that?'

'From the sergeant, the mighty law.'

'The sergeant said that?'

'In so many words.'

She pulls the bedclothes tightly around her.

I glare at her.

'I didn't know, Francis. You must believe that.' Her voice has a strange conviction in it. 'I mean think of it, all you told me yourself, how could one ever be sure with someone like her? I genuinely believed it was George's, although George wouldn't admit it at first, and then, as time went on, I got him to admit it was possible. But why wouldn't I think like that, the way she blackmailed us about the car crash, and knowing that your father would never tell you ...'

'How do you know that?' I say.

'Mrs Dempsey, she ...'

'Ah, Mrs Dempsey.'

'Yes, she told me. But Freddy, he could've been the son of any of the avenue bucks.'

'Shut up,' I say.

'Sorry, Francis,' she says, 'I didn't mean ... I was just glad ...' She's breaking down. 'I was just glad to have him, Freddy I mean, no matter whose he was, but I never counted on getting

187

ill, not long term I mean like this. If I'd known that, maybe...'

'Maybe,' I say, 'all the maybes.'

She brushes a tear aside with the tip of her finger. 'I had such...'

'Expectations?' I say sarcastically.

She sighs. 'Who can ever foretell the way things turn out? But that sergeant... is he a redfaced fella, sort of heavy?'

'What if he is?'

'That's Jack Caffrey,' she says. 'He grew up with George, would you believe it? Oh, a right rake too in his time, until he put on the uniform. He would've known. He would've known all George's little ... indiscretions.'

'But why didn't you tell me something, anything?'

'How could I, Francis? I keep telling you I didn't know the half of what was going on, no more than yourself.'

She looks up at me now wearily. 'And if there is any truth, Francis, that is it.'

'That sergeant was lying,' I say. 'How could Freddy have been my son? Myrtle was already pregnant before she met me. You told me that yourself.'

'That's what I thought, Francis all along. She pulled the wool over all our eyes.'

'Christ.'

I stand stupefied for a moment.

'And I still presumed it was George's,' Noreen continues, 'after the last... after the way things were.'

'She didn't even want her own child.'

'It was her way of getting back at George I suppose for spurning her.'

'You'd think George would've known.'

'George wouldn't have known his own father, Francis. Half his life was an eclipse. With the drink.'

She ponders. 'No, it was all a pretence just to try and get George to marry her, and when he turned her down, she tried the same trick on you, except with you it was for real.'

She looks up at me. 'But it's only now since you told me what

Caffrey said...'

  'It's only now what?' I say

  'It's since I've got to know you more, I can see...'

  'See what?'

  'The resemblance, Francis. I can see Freddy in your face.'

I'm in the library trying to concentrate on the non-fiction, trying to get them in order, exact to their Dewey decimal point. I'm focusing as hard as I can to stop thinking about Freddy, to stop thinking about dividing walls dividing lives, to stop thinking about wallpaper and Freddy, to stop thinking about my father and my mother and George and Myrtle and Freddy and a dog. To stop thinking. To stop going mad.

I put books up on the stacks. I look up dictionaries. I want to find a word for a hater of children and I can't. There must be a word. Hate: *an emotion of extreme dislike or aversion, detestation, abhorrence, the opposite of love: she hated easily, she hated heartily and she hated implacably; to hate to promise much and fail; to hate being bothered.* Maybe it's not hatred of children Myrtle had but *fear* of children. Paedophobia, that'll do.

Michael is working at the desk, putting up a brave front despite the constant worry of not knowing what awaits him every evening when he returns home. Maybe I've succeeded in giving him a little affirmation, I don't know. I wonder really. Maybe Noreen is right, why bother? Why bother with anything? Freddy. Murdered maybe by his half brother for all I know. Christ, it's like a Greek tragedy. Maybe I really am the dismembered statue after all. I'm trying to control a rising anger once more. And then I say why control it? Why don't I just burst in on Myrtle, burst into my own house and catch her *in flagrante* and tear her hair out.

But I realise that's exactly what they would want me to do.

I hear church bells ringing. It must be Sunday again. I've lost track of days. Days just spent moping and musing staring out windows, waiting, trying not to do anything rash. There is no point in taking it out on Noreen. It seems she was caught up in it all just as much as myself. How can I blame her? I've just lit a fire for her and I'm looking out the sitting-room window when I see Father Mack's white Ford Focus driving up towards Mrs Dempsey's bungalow. I jump up suddenly as if something has stung me. I put on a coat and shout up to Noreen that I'll be back soon.

'Francis,' she calls in her weak voice.

'What?' I say rather petulantly, not anxious to go up the stairs.

'Be careful,' she shouts and I wonder how many times that oneliner has been used in Hollywood films. But she means well. I know she's upset by what I have discovered and, strange as it may seem, I think it is genuinely a new discovery for her as well. And I wonder what thoughts flitted silently through her mind as she emptied George's pockets to get his suits drycleaned. All through the years habituating herself to all of that. And now the irony of it all. Now the shock.

I see a young man coming towards me as I walk down the avenue, head lopsided holding his ear, a Swiftian character come to life, from the floating island of Laputa. As he comes nearer I see it is not his ear he is holding but a mobile phone. He is chatting and laughing. Funny that about mobile phones. They make you oblivious of your surroundings. He's looking down, expects me to get out of his way. I want to smash his mobile phone. I stand my ground. He collides into me.

'Hey,' he says.

'Any news?' I say.

'What?'

'From the other world?'

No news from Freddy's world. What number do I need to dial?

I glare at the priest's car in the driveway, as I approach to ring Mrs Dempsey's doorbell. The new bungalow is kept well. White painted walls. Still does her gardening, still planting roses, still seeing the utility in things.

'Francis,' she says as she opens the door.

'I just thought I'd give you a shout,' I say.

'Come in, come in.'

There's a smell of cooking.

'You'll stay for a bite to eat.'

'If there's enough to go around?' I say.

'Of course,' she says. 'Father Mack has just arrived before you.'

I go into the sitting-room where Father Mack is warming his buttocks at a blazing fire. He's drinking a whiskey.

'Ah Francis Copeland, well now,' he says, giving me a big grin. 'It's a long time. You haven't been for a while, have you?'

'Been, Father?'

'To Mass?'

'No,' I say.

Father Mack waits for me to elaborate, to express guilt, to apologise, to make an excuse but I say nothing more on the matter.

Mrs Dempsey comes in carrying steaming plates. We sit at a small table, opposite each other fairly close.

'That looks like a grand bit of roast, Philomena,' Father Mack says.

'It surely does,' I say.

Mrs Dempsey glows. 'It's not much at all. Oh, I forgot to put on the extractor. It's a godsend that. God be with the days in the cottage when I used to leave the door open to let out the steam.'

'And to let the cold in,' says Father Mack giving a grand chuckle.

'Indeed, Father,' says Mrs Dempsey, 'and maybe to let in more than cold. But the electric is great and it's so clean. Do you remember the old hob, Francis?'

'I do,' I say.

'Progress is a wonderful thing,' says Father Mack.

'It surely is,' says Mrs Dempsey on her way out to the kitchen.

'I was sorry to hear about your dad, Francis,' says Father Mack.

'Thank you, Father,' I say.

'He's okay?'

'He's mending.'

'I'm always meaning to get around to see him, but you know how it is in a parish with all the demands that are made on one.'

'Oh, indeed I do, Father.'

'I don't know how he does all he does,' says Mrs Dempsey, coming in with a plate of vegetables. 'It amazes me.'

'Will you go on out of that now, Philomena.'

'Let me get you another little drop, Father, before you start on the dinner.'

'I won't, Philomena. I have to watch the driving.'

'I do forget the new rules. What about you, Francis, you're not driving?'

'I won't, thanks all the same, Mrs Dempsey.'

Father Mack looks at me seriously this time. He lowers his head which forces him to look up over his eyes.

'I've heard about your little trouble,' he says.

'Trouble?'

'With Myrtle. You don't mind my mentioning it?'

'Not at all.'

'She's a good churchgoer, Myrtle.'

'I'll grant you that, Father.'

'Regular in things, Francis.'

'Makes the world go round, Father.'

'I suppose what I'm... we all have arguments from time to time, Francis.'

'Even the cloth, Father?'

'Well I mean...'

'We should grin and bear it, Father, isn't that what you're

saying?'

'Exactly. That's what I was trying to say. She's a good woman, Francis.'

'She is that, Father.'

'No, it's just that...'

'Just what, Father?'

'Well, there's been some talk, and now that I have you here... I hope you don't mind my mentioning it?'

'Talk, you say?'

'About your staying with Noreen Browne, in the same house I mean.'

'I see, Father.'

'It's just maybe if you could... I mean Myrtle and you, it doesn't look good, Francis. If there was any way you could... you know, patch things up?'

'Patch things up. That's a good phrase, Father.'

He stuffs a huge portion of meat and potato between his incisors and chews with his mouth open, showing the food revolving around, and it reminds me of the bin lorry that comes to the avenue.

'Would you mind if I asked you to show me something, Father?'

'What is it, Francis?'

'Would you mind showing me your nails?'

'My nails?'

'Yes.' I laugh. 'I mean on your fingers. I've always admired how clean they were at the altar.'

'Cleanliness,' he says putting down his knife and fork and splaying his hands before me, 'is next to Godliness. You know the saying, Francis?'

'Indeed I do, Father.'

After the meal I say, 'Sure maybe Father Mack would give us an oul song, whenever he's ready.'

'Oh yes,' intones Mrs Dempsey, 'it's ages since you sang for us, Father.'

'Remember the one you had in different languages?' I say.

'Oh, I haven't sung that one in years.'

'What was the name of it, anyway?'

'*Love's Old Sweet Song*, I think if my memory serves me right.'

'Give us a bar now,' I say.

Father Mack takes another sip out of his whiskey, clears his throat and sings:

'Sólo una canción al anochecer
cuando las lámparas...'

'Beautiful,' says Mrs Dempsey as she clears the plates into the kitchen.

'Sorry, Father,' I say. 'Sorry to interrupt, but could you possibly sing it in English this time?'

'In English?'

He looks perplexed.

'Yes. I mean it was originally written in English, wasn't it?'

'Well, yes.' He hesitates for a moment. 'Well, I suppose I could.'

He starts singing in English not quite with the same gusto as he had before:

'Just a song at twilight
when the lights are low ...'

I put my hand under the table and grab his testicles, not taking my eyes off him for a second.

'Lovely, lovely,' I say out loud so that Mrs Dempsey can't hear his grimace from the kitchen.

'Isn't he wonderful, Francis?'

He falters.

'Keep singing,' I say in a low voice, low and threatening, 'keep singing, you bastard,' and I squeeze harder.

'Lovely, lovely,' I say as Mrs Dempsey comes in. His face has gone purple. He has a look of terror now as he sings waveringly and uttering 'Aah' at different ends of the scale and of different intensity depending on the severity of the squeeze. And all the time Mrs Dempsey goes about her chores obliviously.

'Such a beautiful voice,' she says as the priest finishes.

195

'You'll have a little dessert, Francis, a little pudding? Father Mack loves the pudding don't you, Father Mack?'

Father Mack doesn't answer.

'I won't, Mrs Dempsey,' I say quickly filling the void. 'I have to be going now.'

I get up from the table, leaving Father Mack mute and motionless like a statue, except for his colour of course and his contorted face, and the beads of sweat rolling down his bald pate into his pudding.

'Thanks, Mrs Dempsey for a wonderful meal,' I say, and cool as a cucumber I walk out the door.

I'm skimming through some of the more recent books in the library. Funny that, coming across *As if* as a title. Quite arresting. A book by Blake Morrison. That's the way I live my life. As if. That's the way I used to live my life. The alternative reality of vicarious experience always preferred over the other reality, the unprotected reality of hurt and tragedy. Blake Morrison is talking about the tragedy of children who die. As if. Only if. If only. My eyes light up when I read the words: *the dark economy of heaven, so short the path from womb to cloistered tomb* ... The words are making tears roll down my cheeks. I look around to see if anyone has noticed, but there are only a few elderly browsers present, biblebacked over their tomes. *So brief the dolorous stumble* ... Stumble, yes that's what it was, a stumble but a forced stumble ... *from rag-pallet to grave.*

My heart is pounding. The words have done something to me. They have struck a proverbial chord.

I go to the monumentmaker, *Little & Son*, a place near the graveyard that draws you to it by the chip chip sound of a chisel on stone.

The monumentmaker, Mr Little, is an elderly white-haired man.

'I want to change a headstone,' I say. 'There has been a mistake.'

'What?' says Mr Little, lifting up his eyeshield.

I tell him my name. I tell him that Freddy Browne was not Freddy Browne. That he was Freddy Copeland, and when I say it I pause. What a *frisson* the words give. 'Freddy Copeland,' I repeat more for my own benefit than for that of Mr Little. 'I want the record put straight.'

Mr Little scratches his head. 'Jay, that's a strange one, Mr Copeland,' he says. 'In all my years I never heard tell...'

'I'll pay you,' I say, 'whatever it costs.'

'What about the other headstone?' he says, 'the one that's already there.'

'You don't worry about that,' I say.

'And what about the others? The other people?'

'They're dead,' I say.

'Jay, I don't know. What if there's an objection?'

'There won't be,' I say.

'And what did you want to put on the headstone?' he says.

I think for a moment. 'You don't do murder,' I say.

'Jay.' Mr Little draws back. 'What are you saying?'

'Well okay,' I say. 'I want you to put down that Freddy Copeland was the son of Francis Copeland. The lost son. Put that down, the lost son.'

'Copeland,' he says, 'is that with a K or a C?'

'C,' I say. 'And I also want you to put down a little poem.'

'A poem? If there's space,' he says. 'A poem'll cost you extra.'

'That's all right,' I say.

Mr Little writes in a dusty, dog-eared notebook. He writes with the stump of a purple ink-pencil which he keeps dipping on his tongue.

'Oh, one other thing,' I say.

'What's that?'

'I need a loan of your hammer.'

'What?'

'Not the little one,' I say. You do have a sledgehammer?'

'Yes, but...'

I proffer money.

'Don't worry,' I say. 'I'll have it back to you in no time.'

I go into the graveyard. I feel a little apprehensive. I read a notice on the wall of the old disused church. *Reward for information concerning the desecration of monuments. Vandals will be prosecuted.* I look around. There are a number of headstones broken, some bits of stone severed from their sources, strewn on the little path or on someone else's grave. The wrong name. The wrong dead going to the other world like babies mixed up in hospitals, screaming out for their lost kin. I pass a mound of clay, a half dug something or other, an unfinished hole for a plant maybe, too small for a human corpse. I look inside and see an empty cider flagon floating in a pool of water.

I go to Freddy's grave. I look around. There is no one about. I raise the hammer.

Michael is restrained now as he works in the library. No more humming of Beatles' songs, just glum silence, not a bit like his previous self, which sought a chat at every opportunity, despite the restrictive nature of the library code. He's much worse now than when he used to be rejected by his previous girlfriends. He got out of those depressions quickly enough. But this time is different. He's showing a darker side. He is sinking more deeply than ever before with no apparent hope or desire for recovery.

After a few days I say to him, 'This has got to stop, Michael. This is not you.'

'Who else could it be?'

'What's happening, Michael?' I say, thinking that he is still annoyed with me over the ring.

He pushes his glasses up the bridge of his nose, the broken arm held together now with sticking plaster at its hinge.

'You didn't get them fixed?' I say, pointing to the glasses.

'What's the point? Everything's fu ... fucked up.'

'Sit down,' I say. The library is quiet. It's one of these sprawling, anonymous places, unlike my compact library manned by two known persons. Here the staff come and go. There is little friendliness here; it is just an interim place, a place to wait before embarkation, before setting out for somewhere permanent. There are a couple of assistants whom I do not know manning the desk, a girl in jeans and a young man with long hair and open neck shirt. Strict sartorial dictates are no longer binding among library staff. Michael never broke the mould, except the once. He never let his wiry curls grow long. He always wore a tie to the accompaniment of flannels and tweed jacket with leather elbow pads – a true sign of a sedentary lifestyle, or a sign that two stilts are worn thin from trying to hold one's head up in an oppressive world.

I sit Michael down in my temporary, windowless office. There is a smell of old newspapers, of mice droppings, of mildew. It's a place where hand washing is *de rigueur*.

I call the porter, a short stocky fellow who smokes surreptitiously at every opportunity, and I ask him to bring tea.

Michael sits bent forward, eyes to the floor, hands rubbing impatiently together.

'I don't know what to do, Francis.'

'Is it Judy?'

'It's since we mo ... moved in to my mother's house, he's fucking terrifying us.'

Michael's language has coarsened. This is not him.

'Who is terrifying you?'

'Spikey.'

The porter arrives and puts the tea tray on the desk. 'Will I put the friction on the shelves guv, the trolleys are overflowin'?'

'Thank you.'

'Don't mind that bo ... bollocks,' Michael shouts, 'he's just trying to show me up.'

'It's okay,' I say to the porter, 'I'll be out in a minute.' I'm embarrassed for this man who reads fiction as friction. He leaves, looking askance at Michael, and I can't think of his name.

I glance at Michael. I never saw him looking so troubled. 'Drink your tea,' I say.

'Can you get me out of here?' He ignores the tea. 'Can you get me into the Mobile unit or somewhere, anywhere out of this shithole?'

'What is it, Michael?'

'Mam is living in terror. I think her mind is going.'

'How did he ...?

He draws the back of his hand across his brow. 'You see, when we moved in ... I didn't know when I married Judy ... I didn't know.'

'Didn't know what?'

'That Spikey's feeding her drugs, fuck sake. She'll do anything for them, do you hear me, *anything?*'

Tears are filling Michael's eyes, large drops magnified by his lenses.

'Did you ever feel helpless, Francis? Did you ever feel that there is nothing in the world you can do? Ah fuck.'

'Will I go up with you?'

'What?'

'To the house?

'Are you crazy?' He'd knife you. She gets vi ... visitors.'

'What?'

'He keeps watching me, keeps paring his nails with his knife, while Judy is ...' Michael cries out.

'Easy now,' I say.

'I tell you it's hopeless, Francis. I can't go to the gardaí. I'm afraid of what he might do to Mam.' There's a look of heart-rending anguish in his face. 'Francis, you understand wha ... what I'm saying?'

'I understand,' I say.

That's all I can come up with. Just those two words.

I'm worrying about Michael as I lock the library door after me. Never saw him so down before, so completely deflated. *Hopeless*, he kept repeating the word. What is he going home to? What things will he see? Will he be able to endure? What chance does he have alone with his little mother? How far will they drive him? How far did they drive Freddy? They will be too cute for him, those people of the world, just like in a previous time they were too cute for me.

Everything in the grove is quiet. There isn't a stir in the air. The cherry blossoms, skeletal now standing in perfect symmetry in their neat verges, afford me a guard of honour as I pass. The outside light comes on as I approach the house. I ring the bell. Michael's mother shouts from inside. 'Who is it?' 'It's Francis Copeland.' I hear the sound of a mortise lock being opened and a chain being pulled back.

'Oh, Mr Copeland.'

'Francis,' I say.

'How good to see you... Francis.'

She looks worn standing there in a pink cardigan buttoned wrong, her hair uncombed. She cocks her head out the porch and glances up and down the grove anxiously. 'Come in. Come in.'

'I was a bit worried,' I say, 'about Michael. He seemed to be in very bad form leaving work this evening. I just...'

'He went straight to bed. He was exhausted. I hope you don't mind my saying it, Francis, but lately there's been a bit of a strain...'

'Where's Judy?' I say.

She casts her eyes upwards. 'She's out.'

'He didn't look well, Mrs Troy.'

'Oh God,' she cries

'Are you all right?'

She takes a tissue from her sleeve and dabs her eyes. 'What we are being put through!'

'Michael mentioned something. That's why I was worried in case ... You think he's asleep?'

'I don't know. There was some noise but now it's all quiet.'

Suddenly my breaths come quick and short. 'I think we'd better...'

She turns the landing light on, revealing a jagged gap in its glass shade.

'It's the first on the left,' she says.

There is no answer when I knock on the bedroom door. 'Michael, it's Francis.' I open the door and find the light switch. Michael is not there. The bed is made, covered with a cream-coloured quilt. There's a note on the bedside table, it's corner caught by *The Book of Facts* with the words. 'Sorry Mam,' and signed, 'Michael'.

I hand the note to Mrs Troy.

'Oh Francis, what ...?'

'Easy now,' I say trying to calm her.

I go out to the landing. The attic door is open.

'The ladder,' she says, pointing up, 'you pull it down by the cord.'

The light is on in the attic as I pull myself up. It's floored and full of junk rising up to the rafters.

That's where I see him, hanging from a rope.

'What can you see, Francis?' Mrs Troy shouts, coming up a couple of rungs of the ladder.

'Stay down.'

I climb up the junk mountain and, balancing myself precariously on a large suitcase, I lift Michael up to ease the rope off. We both tumble down together.

'What is it, Francis?' Mrs Troy screams. 'What's going on?'

'In a moment.'

There's still warmth in his body like the warmth of the bird that was trapped in Noreen's house. I lay him on his back on the floor. I thump the back of my hand on his chest as I'd read about somewhere, but that was for a drowning, but it's the same thing, isn't it? Whether it's a rope or a fire or an anaesthetic, they're all drownings. I lift his arms up and down as if they are wings trying to restore flight to a bird and then, not without some revulsion, I administer the life kiss.

I watch the chest give a little start like it had got a fright, and his tongue sticks out. I start to count the breaths, short panicky breaths like Melancholy used to have after a run, two or three per second, and I notice his glasses are missing. What a thing to notice at a time like this, and then the breaths slow down and the breathing comes steady and even.

He opens his eyes.

'Oh my God,' cries Mrs Troy, her head peeping through the hole in the ceiling. 'Is he alive?'

'He's all right now,' I say.

'Thank God.'

'You go down. We've had enough accidents for one day.'

I look at Michael. I am angry. I am bloody angry.

204

'What did you try that for?' I say. 'You'd let the bastard do that to you. And your mother? You just bail out, is that it, when the going gets a bit tough, is that it?' I'm shaking him. 'Is that it?' I shout.

'Leave me alone,' he whispers in half strangled words.

'Don't you understand, we can beat them, Michael, but only together. The whole bloody crowd of them; it's all a league – Spikey, Judy, Myrtle, Ida, the whole damned lot.'

'Not Judy.'

'Oh Michael,' I say.

'Do you re ... really think we can beat them?'

'Yes,' I say, 'now where are your glasses?'

'Over there in my jacket.'

The jacket is neatly draped over a tall cardboard box.

'What's the opposite of death, Francis?' he says putting on his glasses.

'Come on now,' I say trying to lift him up. 'That's enough about dying for one day.'

'It's me ... memory.'

'Mind your step,' I say.

'I'm sorry about your mo ... mother's ring, Francis.'

'That's all right.'

'It wasn't Judy. You've got to understand that. It was Spikey's doing.'

'Forget it.'

He pulls at my sleeve. 'You've got to be ... believe that, Francis?'

Mrs Troy shouts from below. 'Is he all right, Francis?'

'He's fine, Mrs Troy. We're coming down.'

Mrs Dempsey is standing at the sink in Noreen's kitchen as I come in. She looks distraught.

'What's wrong, Mrs Dempsey?' I say.

'He's gone, Francis.'

'Who's gone?' I say.

'Father Mack. He's left the parish. He took everything with him. All his things. It's for good this time, Francis.'

'It *is* for good, Mrs Dempsey.'

'What am I going to do at all, Francis?'

At last I see the mortality in her face. She *is* an old woman, suddenly aged in the space of hours. The face shows cracks; the body looks frail. She is supporting herself by gripping the edge of the sink, breathing hard.

'Sit down,' I say, 'I'll make you a cup of tea.'

'He'll be a great loss to the parish.'

'Loss is not the word, Mrs Dempsey.' I say, and I'm conscious of echoing my father's tone from somewhere deep inside me and from long ago.

'And to me, Francis. He'll be a great loss to me.'

'There will be others.'

'Oh God, I don't know anymore. The way the world is going. How is your poor father?'

'Getting better.'

'Someone was praying for him. How long will they keep him in the hospital?'

'Not too long, I hope.'

'I'll have to go in to see him.'

'He'd like that.'

'You know I miss him already. Such a dreadful thing to happen.'

She sips her tea. There's a slight crack in the cup, a hairline fracture.

'The gardaí went up to the canal,' she says. 'Did you hear?'

'No,' I say.

'They wore riot gear. That's what Mrs Carpenter said. The cider-drinkers pelted them with stones, but they broke through their ranks. God forgive me, Francis but I would've loved to have seen some of those gurriers' heads opened. Mrs Carpenter said that the gardaí found drugs and that they made some arrests.'

'Spikey? He was seen?'

'He was seen all right.'

'Did they catch him?'

Mrs Dempsey pauses for a moment, thinking. 'No, not him. I would've remembered if they'd caught him.'

'Will you eat something, with the tea I mean?'

'I'm fine now, Francis, with the cuppa. You know he was fostered?'

'Spikey?'

'Yes. The avenue cares for her own, Francis; least that's the way it used to be, Lord save us. In the old days after a disaster, like a fire or something, if the parents were lost the childer would be fostered out among families. It happened a few times.'

'Without formalities?' I say

'Divil a bit.'

'And who ...?'

'George Browne,' she says. 'He sent him over to the Hanrattys.'

'You're sure he was George's?'

'Oh, he was that.'

'Tell me about the Hanrattys.'

'A strange crowd. Enda Hanratty ...'

'Enda Hanratty?'

'A good friend of George Browne. They drank together, and God knows what else. He agreed to take the child off George's hands. George was always coming and going. He wasn't married then, you understand – not that marriage made much difference to him. Poor Noreen.' She sighs. 'Is she still asleep?'

We listen for a moment. 'Not a sound,' I say.

'I'll check on her in a minute, but I don't know how Hanratty wound up getting him. He said he'd put the child to work as soon as he was big enough, and himself would be able to rest on his laurels. At least that was the story that went around, but how different it all turned out. The funny thing is they got on like a house on fire.'

'A house on fire,' I say.

'Oh, I put me big foot in it there, didn't I Francis,' she says checking herself, 'but you know what I mean?'

'Of course I do, Mrs Dempsey.'

She ponders. 'Maybe there was money involved, some transaction or other, I can't say for certain, not that he deserved any, divil the bit of fostering he did, or the wife either for that matter. She was always off gallivanting, and he practically lived in the Diamond, with the result that the young Philip or Spikey as he later become known, ran wild. Much wilder than Freddy ever was. Up by the canal where the Hanrattys lived was always a tough area. Tougher than the avenue.'

She pauses for a moment, reflecting. 'Funny that.'

'What?' I say.

'No, it's just I'm musing to myself now, Francis. I'm thinking about your father, God be good to him, and I wish him a speedy recovery. But Sam and me, we used always be giving out about the avenue, and here I am now defending it. But that Philip Hanratty fella was bad news from the word go. He always had it in for Freddy.'

'Why was that?' I say.

'I don't know exactly. I think it was the green eye or something. He resented Freddy being in the same house as George. Maybe he knew about his parentage, I can't say, but there was something wrong somewhere right from the word go. And George himself, he resented Freddy being there as well. I remember him boxing Freddy's ears one day when I was in the house and it was all over a comic.'

'A comic?'

'Could you credit it? The poor child was roaring, and he told Freddy to stop wasting time reading, and to go and do something useful, and he boxed him right out the front door.'

Michael is working on the lower stacks. Was always good like that, sensitive; always did the lower stacks in deference to my knee. I'm keeping an eye on him. He's absorbed in his underworld. He looks a bit unkempt. Understandably. A little bristle under his chin – a missed spot; the same shirt as the previous day, a stain on the left lapel of his jacket. All understandable things. Still, he's keeping himself together (I hope). He knows he has to for his mother's sake. 'She hasn't been too well since,' he says when I ask how things are on the homefront. 'It's an ordeal for her too. I realise that.'

I suggested they get police protection, but they're petrified of what Spikey might do. I offered my father's bungalow. 'For a short while,' I said, 'till things blow over (whatever that may mean), until the gardaí get to the bottom of it.' But Michael declined the offer. 'It's vacant,' I said, 'with Dad in hospital. A brand new bungalow.' 'No,' said Michael, 'we've got to stay put. I've got to think of Judy.' 'But she's ...' 'No, No,' he said silencing me. 'I won't leave her.'

You nearly did, I was about to blurt out, but thought twice.

I draw closer to him at the stacks. I know he doesn't want to talk anymore about the homefront, so, partly to distract him, I say to him, 'Any facts on fosterage?'

'Fosterage?' he says, getting up off his knees.

'Ah, I have you there,' I say, having a stab at levity.

'No, no, it's ju ... just I'm thinking.'

Michael takes a reference book from a shelf and starts skimming through it. 'I know it was an important practice in ancient times.'

'Yes?'

'Yes.'

'Tell me more.'

'Ah fuck, here.' His voice is quivering.

'Are you all right?' I say.

'I ju ... just don't feel like ...'

'It's okay,' I say, taking the book with the relevant page open.

Michael goes over to the stampout desk where a queue is forming.

I read the page. Fosterage was a custom dating back to early Celtic society where a prepubescent child was sent to the house of a person talented in some of the arts, and he learned from that person as if he were learning a trade. He would live and study in that house until he reached the age of choice. He would learn many things: music, literature, poetry, the art of warfare, the virtue of single combat, the high value of honour, and how to play chess.

I'm looking out the window of Freddy's room. It's Saturday evening, still light. All the leaves have fallen now. It's just a winter scene, a grey space, a void, just trees standing naked in the cold, as if the world has been skinned and is now being shown raw. It's that time of year every year when I want to run inside the covers of a book. Only now I know I can't.

A squadcar is slowly driving up the avenue. It stops outside Mountain View. The same young garda and bangarda who played ball with the boys on the avenue get out of the car, in full uniform now. Some neighbours and kids gather to watch. The gardaí knock at the front door of my house. While waiting for the door to be answered, the garda looks around. His gaze moves toward Noreen's house, towards the upper windows. He sees me. I feel myself reddening (like when I first saw 'Sandra' in her window), and I pull back.

The gardaí have been admitted. I don't know who admitted them. I missed out on that when I drew back. I hear shouting coming from next door. I hear Ida's and Myrtle's voices. I hear the words 'football' and 'fuck off' and 'prove it' and 'solicitor' and even the name 'Céline' crops up, but I do not hear the voices of the gardaí. And then I hear the sound of footsteps going upstairs.

Some of the kids, John Paul and Tomo among them, are milling around the squad car. A couple of them, shading their eyes with their hands, stare inside, probing the mysteries of the law, while others are stooped, examining the tyres.

The door of Mountain View opens, and Myrtle and Ida are led out. Ida is mouthing something, protesting. The bangarda is carrying two torn plastic footballs.

'What's the commotion?' says Mrs Dempsey, coming into the

room, carrying a mop.

'Nothing much,' I say deadpan. 'It's just my wife and her lover being arrested.'

'Jesus, Mary and Joseph.'

Myrtle looks up and sees me and Mrs Dempsey at the window before she gets into the squadcar. The look says it all. She motions to Ida who looks up also. It's unnerving, but I hold my gaze this time with Mrs Dempsey's hand resting reassuringly on my shoulder. I even try a little smile down at them, for there is nothing either one can threaten me with now, no scissors or shears or steam iron, nothing but clenched fists straining powerlessly through handcuffs.

The window is open so I can hear John Paul and Tomo and Sue Ellen (getting one back for her sister) boo the women and shout, 'Ballcutters out,' as they are ushered into the squadcar. And as the squadcar hobbles off with diminished air in it tyres, there is a great hooray and clapping from all the kids.

Mrs Dempsey presses tightly on my shoulder. 'God forgive me, but I'm glad too, Francis,' she says. 'She was never right for you.'

I'm back in my own house once more. My own house with new locks (that might be an interesting name, New Locks, to replace Mountain View). I tear off the bedclothes from the 'matrimonial' bed. I pull down the GROW YOUR OWN DOPE sign from the bedroom wall and the Mountain View name from the porch, and assign them with the bedclothes to the dustbin. I open all the windows of the house. But there's a lingering smell. I'm convinced it's that of Ida. She's ingrained in the wood, in the walls, in the carpets. Ida is everywhere.

I go to work in the early light. I try to talk to Michael in the library, but he has imprisoned himself in his own world and hardly bids me the time of day. He expects me to say Judy is fine, Judy is wonderful, but both of us know she's a junkie; he won't admit, innocently or not, that it was she who brought him to this impasse.

I come home in the darkness. I call to Noreen. She has finished *The Age of Reason* and is now into *Nausea*. I bring her tea and toast. She is still ill of course. She is still dying, but her dying is as long as some people's living. And although she's kind to me and sympathetic, I feel I'm distancing myself from her more and more. It's not just because of her coming on to me, or her using me as a sounding board for her pent-up vulgarisms. Perhaps it's more to do with the feeling of perpetual sameness which she engenders, a world of unending gloom. Perhaps it's due to all the years spent with my father. Although I feel sorry for her, to take another dejected person on board is too much, too hard to handle. Perhaps smaller dollops of misery administered more randomly, maybe that, I could manage

I enter my own house. The air inside is cold. It's not worth

214

lighting a fire. It's too late. No one to share it with anyway. I go to bed, covering myself with my coat (I didn't buy new bedclothes yet). I'm going to break up this bed. I'm going to burn it on a bonfire. The wind is rising outside. It blows through the empty house, through all the cavities in windows and doors. The house is a hollow vessel, just like my father's mind. There are no books near my bed. They're still in their boxes. Sometimes there's no escape from things. Sometimes there is only one world.

Then I say to myself the house may be a hollow vessel, but it's mine. Number forty eight. Bingo!

I'm drawn to the grove like a moth to lamplight. I'm near Michael's house. How can I help him? I'm hovering around, hoping that proximity will endow me with some inspiration. What is the nightmare? Is it the same one every night? Judy is in there I know, and Spikey most likely, and Michael's mother incarcerated in a room perhaps.

I see Enda Hanratty walking up the grove. He doesn't see me standing in the shadows of a denuded prunus. He opens Michael's gate. He pulls his coat collar up around his ears before knocking at the door. Spikey's face appears in the slit opening. Enda gives a half glance behind before slipping in.

I walk away. I could report them but it could implicate Michael, and even his mother, as the owners of a house of ill-repute.

I meet John Paul and Tomo as I return to the avenue. They are getting increasingly angrier about Spikey.

'We can't play ball anymore,' says John Paul.

'There's not a ball that's not burst,' says Tomo. 'He comes along every time we are playin' and grabs the ball from us. He rips it apart with his knife and looks inside as if expectin' to find somethin'.'

'The fuzz do the same,' says John Paul.

'Yeah, and we thought there would be no more of that with the ballcutter gone,' says Tomo.

'The bollockses,' says Tomo.

Spikey. The cops can't nab him. He's the pimp in the elusive pimpernel. He's up in that house in the grove, feeding Judy's habit, keeping her in thrall, maintaining a steady flow of sex and smack and maybe even slow murder. Perhaps a syringe with an air bubble for Michael's mother. Or maybe he's

216

preparing *Hot Knives* – I read about that: heating resin with a knife on the ring of a cooker, forcing them to knock it back with a slug from the brown flagon.

'I know where Spikey is,' says John Paul. 'I know what he's doin' up in the grove.'

'Sellin' sex with your one.'

'Me oul fella went to her.'

'The fuckin' avenue's ridin' her.'

'They're holding an old woman in the house,' I say.

'Get the fuzz.'

'Fuck the fuzz,' says Tomo. 'We've got to think of a plan.'

'What can we do, Franky?' says John Paul.

I move away. 'Catch you later,' I say.

'Are you goin', Franky?'

'We'll talk later.'

Need to clear the head, need to walk. And then I remember Ida's phrase: *use what you have to get what you want.*

I walk around the back of the avenue. I knock at Dorothy's door. I'm not sure why I'm doing this. It's a sort of impulse. It's like your mind is saying, *Do something while I'm on hold. I'll get back to you as soon as I can.* Perhaps Dorothy can help. Surely, despite everything, a mother's care ... surely maternal instincts are stronger than all that's right or wrong. But then look at Myrtle. Still it's worth a try.

'Who's there?' Dorothy shouts from inside. Not the usual chirpy Dorothy, a note of fear in her voice.

'It's me,' I say, 'Francis Copeland.'

'What do you want?' she says gruffly.

'I want to talk to you about your daughter.'

'She's not here.'

'I know. That's why I want to talk to you.'

Dorothy opens the door. She's in her dressing gown. Her hair is wet and she's holding a towel. 'I know you know things,' she says. 'I know you saw me in the factory. You were with Michael, but I have to ask you a question.'

'Okay.'

'Did you say anything to him, I mean about ...?

'No,' I say, 'I'm not here about that.'

She opens the door wider to let me in to the darkened hall. My foot collides with a suitcase.

'You're going somewhere?' I say.

'I might be.'

Dorothy sits me down in a pink settee opposite a wall with a picture of a female nude. She goes out for a moment and comes in with a brandy in a large brandy glass. 'Here you are, lurve.' It's a generous measure. 'Sorry for being gruff there,' she says sitting down in a one-seater opposite me. 'It's just I'm a little edgy these days with the arrests and all.' Then looking at the carpet, she says, 'I know about Ida and your wife. I'm sorry about that. Always was. Never agreed with that sort of thing, you know.'

'It doesn't matter now,' I say.

'I know she's my sister and everyone has their own orientation and all that, lurve – I never saw her growing up, you know; she was just a nipper when I had to leave for England. But I don't like seeing a marriage being broken up when it can be avoided that is, not that I can afford to talk, mind. And Judy, I know what you're going to tell me about Judy?'

'You do?'

'She's gone to the bad again, hasn't she?'

She moves her hands, putting one on top of the other. 'I know what you're thinking, lurve, that I encouraged it. I'll be honest with you. I had no objection to pulling an odd trick myself when I was across, independent like. I had no choice. We got no maintenance from Paddy.'

'Paddy?'

'Me permanently-pissed husband. He's probably lying in a Liverpool gutter at this moment. I mean, don't get me wrong, when we came over here I played me part in the operation.'

'I know,' I say.

'I won't deny it, but I never thought of Judy getting hooked. It doesn't hit you until you see one of your own. I didn't allow for

218

that. That was all Spikey's doing to get the power. And me own sister knows and never lifts a finger to help.'

'Do you want to break them up?' I say.

'Break them up?'

'Yes.'

'That's what I was trying to do by getting her married to Michael. Spikey has fucked her up. He's fucked us all up. Excuse me French, lurve, but Judy was all right you know before she met him.'

'You worked for Spikey,' I say.

'The bastard,' she says, 'he owes us money, and Judy, you should see the way he treats her.'

'Where can we hit him?' I say.

'What?'

'His weakness.'

'Oh, cider without a doubt, lurve. Even though he shoots up he's not an addict. Too bleedin' cute. He gets others hooked, that's his style, but he becomes certifiable if he doesn't have his flagon.'

I skim through detective books in the library. Never bothered reading them before. Lots of moral rot, someone said; I think it was DeLillo. I always found them too formulaic, but now I'm looking for a formula. Chandler, Christie, Wilkie Collins' *The Woman in White*, still being borrowed.

A young man hands me a membership form. He is one of the Bosnian refugees.

'Are you a householder?' I say.

'Pardon, sir?'

'Do you own a house?'

'No, sir.'

'You have to have it signed by the owner of a house.'

The young man is about to walk away. 'Don't you live near me?' I say. 'On the avenue?'

'Yes, sir. There was a fire in the library up there. That is why I ...'

'I can sign it for you. I'm a householder.'

'May I take a book out now?'

'Of course,' I say.

'This one.'

He hands me a book on suburbia by Ethel Longworth Smith. I scan through the pages: 'Those whose eyes light to see a swirl of dry leaves in the autumn... thank that enterprising realtor, Babbitt, for the suburbs.'

'May I have my book now, sir?'

'Sorry,' I say. I stamp his book. 'You're interested in the suburbs?'

'Yes, sir.'

'You're going to stay here then, in this country I mean?'

'Oh yes.'

I bid him good day and return to the stacks. Back to where I was. Danger is sanitised in the world of detective fiction. It's just a game, a little puzzle to solve, the same as doing a crossword or a Rubik's cube. If life is a puzzle, as my father maintained, then it too can be solved.

Spikey struts out of the off-licence with the flagons protruding out of a brown paper bag. Tomo and John Paul and a few of the other, bigger kids of the avenue are waiting with me in a darkened shop doorway opposite the No Ice, watching the cider-drinker come out.

Spikey goes up to his 'wheels' which are positioned at the side of the off-licence. He places the bag on the ground so that he can put on his helmet. That's when John Paul and Tomo pounce. I had told them that cider could be Spikey's undoing, and if they took it away from him, he would be certifiable. I told them that it would be like taking away the hair of Samson. They did not know what that meant, so I told them it meant that if he hadn't got his cider, he would go crazy and would have to be put away. They thought that a great plan, and said, 'Thanks, Franky, we knew you wouldn't let us down.'

Spikey is shouting, looking for his cider. Someone throws a stone and hits the cider-drinker on the side of his face. He shakes his fist at shadows. He fumes; he rants and raves under the street lamp; he wheels around in circles. 'Someone will pay,' he shouts, holding the side of his face, 'some of you fuckin' avies.' He tries unsuccessfully to catch the strap of his helmet. I lipread an expletive. I see his black leathered buttocks extend as he mounts his mechanical steed and revs nerveshatteringly, leaving a trail of smoke behind him as he drives towards the avenue.

We head back, chameleons of darkness. We mock the lights of Spikey's machine. We taunt silently from our secret places as the metal animal becomes frenetic and snarls up and then down the avenue, a wild beast unable to ensnare its prey.

And for a moment, fleeting, George Browne's death passes

before my eyes.

A squadcar coasts by, its headlights strobing the avenue.

'Get down,' says John Paul.

We crouch down against the Carpenters' gable-end wall.

'They got the English one's mother,' whispers Tomo.

'When?' I say.

'Today,' says Tomo. 'They nabbed her at the airport.'

'How do you know that?' I say.

'Me oul fella works out there. He saw her being arrested when she was trying to board a plane.'

The boys whisper as if they are involved in some great conspiracy. 'Thanks, Franky. Thanks, Franky,' they say, and start to open the flagons.

'Hold on, lads,' I say. 'I don't want you drinking.'

'Why, Franky?' whispers Tomo.

'Why? Because we're crusaders,' I whisper back.

'Crusaders?'

'Like knights, you know.'

'Knights of the Round Table?'

'Exactly. And we need our wits about us.'

'Ah fuck,' says John Paul.

'You want to get Spikey?' I say.

'We do. We do,' they chorus in an affected whisper as loud as ordinary speech.

'Okay, Franky,' says Tomo, surrendering the flagons. 'Once we get *him*.'

I am walking towards the grove, following a distant scream. A scream that penetrates every pore, every wall of every house, every chimney, every window, whether open or closed, every door, every car or truck that passes on the road going north to avoid the toll, and through all of suburbia, the scream can be heard like that of some ancient town crier warning of impending doom.

As I get closer to the grove, I hear doors slamming and bolts closing, and the patter of feet scurrying like frightened rats.

The grove puts me in mind of a ghost town in a Western, empty except for a few season-defying leaves herded along by the wind. The street lamps give out their silent glow. Everywhere is silent apart from that scream, the silence enhancing that sound, making one focus on that one spot which is Michael's house.

I see Enda Hanratty running out of the garden. He is trying to push his shirt down his trousers as he runs. 'She's gone fucking mad,' he shouts. I watch him shifting down the road, growing smaller, disappearing into shadows.

Blinds and curtains are parting slightly in windows. Eyes are following every movement in the street.

I hear the squadcar siren and the *weehoo weehoo* of the ambulance coming closer, both arriving together and screeching to a halt outside Michael's house. I watch the blue light on the roof of the squadcar going round and round.

I hear doors opening. The patter of shoes or high-heels ringing on the pavement, and slippers almost silent like souls shuffling along, all converging on Michael's garden. I see the starers, their voices starting up, whispering at first, tentative and then growing in volume until the area is surrounded by a din.

Two ambulance men bear a stretcher out of the house, carrying a body covered by a sheet from head to toe, covered except for the slight protuberance of a black leather sleeve.

'That's him,' shouts a woman in curlers with her nightdress showing under an overcoat. It's the brolly woman without her brolly now. She recognises me. 'Hello, love,' she says. 'There's one that's done with wondering.'

'He got his comeuppance,' some man shouts.

I go towards the house. I'm told by a sergeant to stand back out of the way. It's Sergeant Caffrey from the station.

'Ah, Mr Copeland,' he says, suddenly recognising me. 'I think we're too late.'

The door of the house opens and Michael's mother is wheeled out in a wheelchair, a rug around her legs. She is wearing a dark woollen coat and hat, and of course her spectacles, and is holding her handbag on her lap. She smiles inanely as she is wheeled by, nodding mechanically like a toy car dog in motion.

Judy and Michael, with his arms protectively holding a blanket over her shoulders, are led out of the house by a garda and bangarda. They pass near me clearly visible under the light. Michael sees me but doesn't speak. Judy stares vacantly ahead. Her hair is matted; there is congealed blood on her hands, and her mouth, hanging open, reveals – something I hadn't noticed before – a rot in her teeth.

Things are returning to normal at last, if normal is the word. I'm back in my study reading, trying to finish *The Name of the Rose* which I had abandoned for a while. Where was I? I was past the abyss. But I can't concentrate, not like before, even though the house is quiet now, except when Dad is dawdling about. He has been discharged from the hospital. They didn't keep him that long at all. A robust constitution, imagine, that's what a doctor said about him. Anyway, he's staying with me now. I'm looking after him again, like old times. (We can decide what to do about the bungalow at some later stage). He's got some new medication from the hospital that's supposed to slow down the senility. And he's taking herbs: St. John's Wort, and Ginkgo Biloba, which Mrs Dempsey swears by. There isn't that much looking-after to do, not really like old times. I arranged for the community minibus to call to forty eight to collect him for his meals in the Centre, where he meets up with some other old timers. Whether there is communication or not, I cannot tell. Maybe the old have their own codes, but at least it's a break for him, and it saves me from washing all those meal plates again. And I have an arrangement made with Mrs Dempsey to look in on him when I'm at work.

We go for walks the two of us – he has a stick now – on a Saturday or Sunday afternoon.We go down by the canal when it's bright and there's no threat of rain, or no threat from the cider-drinkers (most of them have dispersed now with their leader gone). We go to see the wild flowers coming into bloom or watch the swans who have come back, or maybe they're not the same ones. One day we're walking and I discover wild lilac in bloom. 'Look Dad,' I point, 'the lilac,' and I know I'm right this time. He sinks his nose into the fragrance. A hint of a smile. At least one sense intact.

Another day we go up to Mam's grave where we plant dahlia tubers from Dad's old garden. Well, I plant them and he helps. He makes the hole with his stick. 'That's right Dad, very good, just a little bit deeper now,' I say, helping him to push the stick down. 'We don't want the frost getting at them now, do we?' And knowing he can't hear me, I say, 'Let's keep a few for Freddy.' And then I steer him to Freddy's grave which is nearby. I look at my surname, and Freddy's, and Dad's, which is up on the gravestone. But of course Dad is not taking it in. 'The name, Dad,' I say, pulling at his sleeve, 'Copeland, you see?' I point at the letters. 'You had a grandson. A grandson,' I repeat, and I write the word down in his notebook. He looks at it, not understanding, but at least I take satisfaction in knowing it is recorded. He points at a tuber I'd planted crooked, and he kneels down stiffly to adjust it so its little green stalk is pointing upwards. He firms the soil around it with his hand, raking the loam with his nails. On Freddy's grave.

My father used to speak of the waste of fresh flowers on a grave, filling the mourners with sweet smells, and then after a few days ironically seeing them being cleared by grave attendants wearing anti-pollen masks. He considered cut flowers as amputations. He said one shouldn't cut things off from their source, and maybe he was thinking of his cottage as well. That's why even when I cut the rose for Myrtle, I never told him. My father never knew how that affair blossomed.

Speaking of which, Myrtle and Ida were found guilty of drug-trafficking and given seven years. What do I feel about that? Nothing. Not a thing. It's just matter-of-fact like when I brought the smack down to the garda station. At least that's what I keep telling myself. And if I say it often enough, surely it must be true. Dorothy was found guilty of abetting and given three years, but then she got an extra two for procuring. Sergeant Caffrey gave evidence and said he wished to take the opportunity – echoed by the judge – to thank all the good citizens who had carried out their civic duties in reporting incidents, thus expediting the enforcement of the law. Expediting. *That's a good one, Franky.* Judy was found guilty of manslaughter, but when the history was revealed, when it was proved that it was self-defence, that Spikey was coming at her with his knife, she got off scot-free, that is if a detox clinic is *free*. Michael testified in support of Judy. Mrs Troy was also meant to take the stand, but her mind has gone a little woozy, at least that's how Michael put it. 'It's after all she's been through,' he said. 'It's only a temporary thing.' But I don't know. I'm not so sure. All I can say is that she's not the same woman she was before the rope went around her son's neck.

But Michael is in great form. He hums all the time back in our own restored library now. He looks up and quotes from all the books he can find on drugs and addiction, becoming quite an authority in that area. 'She's making progress,' he says to me about Judy. 'The methadone is working. But do you know what the important thing is, Francis?' he says. 'What's that?' I say. 'She *wants* to get well. *Herself*, Francis.' 'You must really love her,' I say, 'I mean after all that's happened?' 'Oh I do, Francis,' he says, smiling, and adjusting his mended glasses on the bridge of his nose.

Back at forty eight, at New Locks (I've put up the name), I attempt to resume my reading, trying to get back to my former routine. But I remember promising Noreen that I'd bring her some new French books from the library. I read a few paragraphs, and then I think of Mrs Dempsey and wonder how she'll get on with the new parish priest who has recently been installed. Myself and Dad are invited around to meet him for Sunday lunch. But I must get back to my reading. I really have to concentrate. I think of the Chinese proverb which says that three days without reading makes talk flavourless. I used to substitute *life* for *talk*.

There's a knock at the front door.

'Sorry, Franky.' It's John Paul and Tomo.

'It's the ball ...'

'It went around the back.'

'It's all right, lads,' I say, 'I'll get it for you.'

I go out the back and get the ball and return it to them.

'It was as high as Freddy's kick,' John Paul says.

'No,' says Tomo. 'It could never be as high as that.'

'Wasn't it, Franky? Wasn't it as high as Freddy's?'

'I don't know, lads,' I say, 'I didn't see it,' and I begin to feel a little breakdown in my voice.

I watch them play for a while. Listen to their voices, muted, almost monotone, missing the high pitched soprano to make their cantata complete. I look at the leafless trees standing like a silent audience in the auditorium of the world. I feel cold. I look at Noreen's house, all quiet, and the pylon opposite with its railing that came too late.

I go back to my study to try to resume my reading (I've lost my page), when I hear Mrs Dempsey's animated voice calling, 'Francis, Francis.'

She comes in with Dad trailing.

'I must've left the door on the latch,' I say.

'Sam let me in. He saw me through the window.'

'You've his notebook there,' I say, noticing her holding it, and Dad has what looks like a cheque in his hand.

'Yes,' she says, 'the post came.'

'I didn't hear it,' I say.

'Great news, Francis,' she says. 'He's got a cheque from the Tontine. It's for you. He wants you to have it.'

I look at Dad. There is no hint, no sign, just a stolid expression.

'How do you know that?' I say to her.

She opens the notebook. 'Read it,' she says excitedly.

They're standing beside each other, the two of them, waiting for me to read. They look like old lovers, a twinkle and a tear. I open the notebook. It's Dad's scrawl all right, unmistakably (with a big bit of help from Mrs Dempsey no doubt).

Just three words: *For the years*.

Acknowledgements

The author wishes to acknowledge the translated extract from Rainer Maria Rilke's *Autumn Day* by Desmond Fennell, and the quote on page 197 from Blake Morrison's *As If* (Granta Books, 1998).

LaVergne, TN USA
01 July 2010
188110LV00001B/39/P